THE MOERS MURDERS

Master Mercurius Mysteries
Book Eight

Graham Brack

Also in the Master Mercurius Series

Death in Delft

Untrue Till Death

Dishonour and Obey

The Noose's Shadow

The Vanishing Children

The Lying Dutchman

Murder in Maastricht

THE MOERS MURDERS

Published by Sapere Books.

224 Trafalgar Road, Ilkley, LS29 8HH,
United Kingdom

saperebooks.com

ISBN: 978-0-85495-515-2

PROLOGUE

I am not one for blowing my own trumpet, but I think I may fairly claim that the tale I am about to tell may be one of the great achievements of my life. [Van der Meer, you are meant to be writing this down; yes, including the trumpet bit; and you can stop raising those eyebrows.]

If I have maintained a natural reticence about these events, it is partly because I am aware that there are still some people so aggrieved by what went on in those distant days that anyone who played any part is still in danger from adherents of one side or the other. However, a number of memoirs have been published in the intervening period that seem to me to be deficient exercises aimed at aggrandizement of some person or other, and you will look in vain for any mention there of my crucial role in safeguarding the interests of my country and, indeed, the peace of Europe. [Van der Meer, I think we might capitalise that phrase — the Peace of Europe.]

It is time to set the record straight. Unlike the other chroniclers, I will freely accept that there are parts of the story I do not know. Some of it had taken place before I became involved so I am dependent on the recollections of others, and one or two men who might have given valuable insights into the plans of the great rulers of Europe have been unable to do so on account of being dead. Nevertheless, I will make the best fist I can of explaining William III's plan for world domination (and why it did not entirely come off), what was going through what — for want of a better word — I will call Louis XIV's 'mind', and why James II of England did not defend his throne but then invaded his own country with foreign help in the hope of displacing his own daughter and son-in-law.

A word of explanation. At various points in the narrative the reader will find me living a life of luxury, bedecked in gold and compelled to drink fine wines. This was not my choice. It was all part of the master plan [Van der Meer, capitalise that too — the Master Plan] to ensure the independence of the Dutch Republic and the continued benevolent rule of William, our Stadhouder.

In the course of this book you will find some old friends and acquaintances and meet some new ones, such as Everhard van Weede van Dijkvelt, normally known as Dijkvelt (actually he was normally known as something else, but one cannot put words like that in a serious work without having it seized and burned by the authorities) who usually gets the credit for all this. I can be magnanimous and allow that he played a part; quite a big part, actually, and he was one of the cleverest, or at least the craftiest, men I have ever known. Dijkvelt was a silver-tongued diplomat so good at his job that if your daughter had been kidnapped and sold into whoredom he could convince you that it was all geared towards making her financially independent.

Since I began publishing these memoirs I have received a large number of gratifying letters from well-wishers expressing their admiration and asking various questions. I have, of course, written back, but one or two enquiries may have a general interest, so I shall answer them now.

J.V. is surprised that I do not use some of my wealth to buy myself a horse and save myself so much walking. I take the point, but there is difficulty in finding places in Leiden to park a horse. On top of that, I regularly travel by barge, and trying to get a horse on a barge is awkward, not to mention that some bargemasters will refuse to take them, the scoundrels! After all, a man who has a horse is clearly a man of substance and therefore not to be spoken to in a vulgar manner by a mere bargemaster.

Mevrouw D. asks whether I will ever marry. It is kind of her to enquire, and to include the information that she is 'a lusty widow-woman in her prime' and has her own pig. One can never say never, but I am now eighty-three years old and very comfortable in my bachelorhood. Of course, one has had one's opportunities but I cannot discuss them here because Van der Meer dribbles over the pages when he gets excited.

The Reverend Dr S. P. v. d. L. takes me to task for involving myself in worldly matters when there is so much to be done in the Church, to which I plead that my involvement in all these cases was involuntary. I never sought to be used in this way and deflected from my duties at my beloved University of Leiden. Nothing would have pleased me more than to live a peaceful life as a lecturer in moral philosophy, researching in the library and teaching in the university, enlightening the students (if indeed it is possible to enlighten most undergraduates, which I increasingly doubt).

A number of correspondents express sympathy for Van der Meer. He does not need sympathy, but a kick up the backside. Despite his deficiencies, I give him steady work by which he can keep his children clothed and fed. I like to think that I am a civilised and progressive employer. Only the other month I gave him a whole day off when his youngest child was baptised. Besides, if he is dissatisfied in any way he can always go and find a job with someone else, so the fact that he stays is testimony to the healthy state of our relationship.

Anyway, this is the story of how I spent far too long travelling, looking important and trying to work out what was going on in the year of 1688. I hope you enjoy it more than I enjoyed living through it.

Leiden, The Feast of St Mary Magdalene de' Pazzi, 1722

CHAPTER ONE

It is, of course, a great sin to rejoice at the misfortune of others, but when I heard that Albrecht, the kitchen master at the university, had injured his arm and would be unable to cook for a while (I use the word "cook" in its loosest sense where Albrecht is concerned) I cannot deny that my heart gave a little skip. Albrecht is a man who can flambé a salad, so his indisposition held out the prospect of edible food for a few weeks, especially given that his wife Mechtild has an angel's touch with pastry. She is not what one could call a dainty woman, but those chubby fingers can perform miracles of the baking art.

Having said that, she was now doing the work of two, as well as having to feed a husband with an arm in a splint, so she was under some strain. It was no surprise, therefore, when she asked if I had an hour or two to spare to help her. Readers who have learned of my previous culinary efforts will be relieved to know that this assistance did not involve doing anything in the kitchen, but in the garden, where the first soft fruit was ripening but needed picking before the birds took all the best for themselves. In exchange for this service, I was promised a selection of tartlets. It is a great shame that Mechtild did not live sixteen hundred years ago, because if Our Lord had tasted her strawberry tart I am fairly sure he would have ordered some for the Last Supper and we would now be dividing a tasty dessert at Holy Communion rather than bread.

I took my bowl and began picking, kneeling on a small board she had given me to protect my clothes, when I saw something that reminded me of yet another blessing. It is possible that I may have mentioned Friedrich Spanheim the Younger in these pages. Despite the evidence of two previous terms of office, he had been re-elected Rector of the university in 1687, replacing my dear friend Johannes Voet. Spanheim was described as a conservative, which was a generous appellation for one of the staunchest Calvinists I ever had the misfortune to encounter.

A tip to the reader: always beware of a man called "the Younger". They automatically feel driven to outdo their elder namesake and go through life bearing grudges. Anyway, the cause for rejoicing was that Spanheim's term of office had not been renewed, despite his mentioning to just about everyone he met that he would be prepared to continue as Rector, and Spanheim had retired to his study to compile his *Collected Works*, a boon for scholars who would now be able to ignore all his writings in one place instead of having them scattered amongst several volumes. Unfortunately, he still had not issued this magnum opus when he died in 1701, so several of his friends subscribed to have an edition published as a mark of respect to his memory. If I had had my way, a volume would have been placed on his chest when he was buried, which should have ensured that he would not rise from the grave to haunt us, but the mammoth tome was not ready in time so the chance was lost. I did, incidentally, subscribe to the volume myself. One cannot expect forgiveness oneself if one cannot forgive others.

His replacement was Charles Drelincourt, who had also served as Rector before. Drelincourt was a Frenchman, but we did not hold that against him. He was also a very skilled physician and surgeon, a highly accomplished classicist who could tell you that you were dying in a range of ancient tongues, and a man of some taste and elegance. On this particular morning I glanced up from my fruit-picking to see

Drelincourt descend from his carriage and then offer a hand to his equally elegant wife Susanna so that she might do the same. She carried a beautiful light blue parasol that matched her summer dress perfectly, and I could see similar bows on her shoes as she raised her skirts above the dirt of the garden to join her friends for a day of shopping.

I may need to explain to gentlemen readers that "shopping" is a very different thing from "going to market". Every family goes to market to buy the things they need, and does so as expeditiously as possible. Ladies of quality, however, go "shopping", which, so far as I can make out, involves meeting your friends for a dish of tea or coffee and then promenading around town talking to people and occasionally going into shops, looking at and perhaps buying a number of things that you do not strictly need. It seems that the time devoted to this is not proportionate to the cost of the item. Whereas a man might buy a horse in an hour, a woman can take three weeks to choose a pair of gloves or a ribbon for a hat.

I was so busy ruminating on this that I completely failed to notice Drelincourt sneaking up on me until he bellowed at me from above:

'Don't we pay you enough, Mercurius? Do you need a second job now?'

I could have told the truth, but this was not the time, I judged.

'No, Rector, this is not to do with pay. This is voluntary work to assist our cook, Mechtild.'

'The under-cook,' Drelincourt corrected me. 'How is her husband?'

'I think his arm is still giving him some pain,' I answered.

'That's not surprising. It was a nasty break.'

I had forgotten that Drelincourt himself had set the bone after Albrecht had fallen off a ladder while trying to lift down a heavy silver platter. There had been a formal dinner at the university that evening so Drelincourt had been dining in, which meant he was only a few dozen paces away when Albrecht hit the ground with a loud crack.

'He is hopeful that he will be cooking again soon,' I added.

'Oh dear,' said Drelincourt. 'I've kept him on full pay to try to ensure that he has no reason to rush back.'

Unlike some Rectors, Drelincourt chose to live out but dine in regularly. This was both to foster a team spirit amongst the staff and, I imagine, some kind of mortification of the flesh to compensate for past sins. For just a few moments I had a ghastly vision of Hell in which the residents were compelled to eat Albrecht's cooking without end, while he exulted in having finally managed to get his oven as hot as he wanted.

'Do you have any plans for the summer, Mercurius?'

'I'm staying here, Rector,' I answered. 'I don't have any family to go to, and I'm hoping to get some more work done on my *Commentary on the Nicomachean Ethics*, Volume Three.'

'Ah, indeed,' said Drelincourt. 'Some day I must catch up with the first couple of volumes.'

I knew he had copies on his shelves. I had given them to him as I had to Johannes Voet; but while Voet's copies were looking rather dog-eared and there were slips of paper inserted at various places, Drelincourt's were pristine.

'And what of you, Rector?' I asked.

'I'm not sure yet,' he answered. 'My wife had thought to visit some of her family in France, but in the current ferment I am not sure that it will be possible.'

Tensions between the Dutch Republic and France were in the air. Louis XIV had passed some decrees inhibiting Dutch trade to France which had proved very damaging to the merchants in Amsterdam, much of whose custom was in fancy goods exported to Paris. Moreover, there were worrying stories of French Protestants like Drelincourt being detained on re-entering France and required to convert to Catholicism or face an indefinite period in jail. In ordinary times Drelincourt, as a former French Army surgeon and a man of considerable reputation, would have been in no danger, but the news from France suggested that Louis was going out of his way to pick a fight with someone, and if it could not be England, it would have to be us.

I say that war with England was unlikely because the King of England, James II, was a firm friend of France and of Catholicism. In the fickle way that absolute rulers have, Louis had suddenly stopped hating England and promoted her to the top of his list of friends when James came to the throne after his brother Charles died. I had met them both. Charles was not particularly religious, fond of port and good living, and had bedded mistresses in most of the stately homes of England, but I quite liked him. He pretended to be a pleasure-loving political innocent when in fact he was a pleasure-loving political operator of the highest order. He was also rather cleverer than both his father and his brother.

On the other hand, although James was a Catholic, I did not warm to him. He always bore that air that afflicts some younger brothers — not me, of course — of being the favourite child and expecting to get his own way just *because* it was his own way. I must allow that his feeling for me seemed equally dismissive, possibly because he saw me as a Protestant minister who had been sent to verify the Protestant orthodoxy of his daughter and did not know that I was, in fact, a secret Catholic.

Ah, now I forgot to mention that. In 1664 I had converted to Catholicism and been ordained as a Catholic priest, but my bishop was concerned that there was persecution in the Low Countries and therefore he wanted some secret priests to build a new church if the old one was ever wiped out. He thus instructed me to keep my Catholicism to myself, an order which suited me very well because it meant I could go on being a lecturer at Leiden, something that would have been out of the question in the Faculty of Theology had it been known.

Occasionally people say to me, 'But by the 1680s surely it was obvious that no repression was likely? William III was very tolerant in matters of religion. He didn't even expel Jews, and that was extremely unusual in Europe then.' That is all true. William positively encouraged Jews to come, particularly if they had money. In return for being left in peace the Jews of Amsterdam were among his most ardent supporters and regularly found reasons to give him a present; his birthday, the anniversary of his institution as Stadhouder, his wife's birthday, his favourite horse's birthday, and so on.

The Catholics did not follow suit. If anything, they kept harking back to the restoration of old privileges like a Catholic university, public processions in our larger cities on Holy Days and sending their children to study in France or Italy. As a result, William did not repeal anti-Catholic legislation. It was not enforced, but it still existed as a reminder to uppity Papists that a step too far could start the bonfires again.

For this reason I took the view that I would keep my secret as ordered by the bishop until such time as he expressly ordered me not to do so. Since the bishop who ordained me had died, as had his successor, and the current incumbent, Pierre Vandenperre, had not written to me for nearly four years, I lived in hope that the order would not come.

Back in 1664 the idea of being the saviour of the Holy Roman Church in the Low Countries when other priests had been arrested or incinerated quite appealed to the romantic side of my nature, but now I could not help thinking that if the reason for disclosing my ordination was that Catholic priests were being immolated all around me, declaring my priesthood was something of a self-limiting career move, and while my faith was strong I was less sure that I had made a wise bargain. Admittedly if I had announced myself as a Catholic I would have been dismissed by the university and possibly expelled from the United Provinces, but the Church would have found me a job somewhere. The snag was that it might have been in France, and I had already been to France. It is even worse than England in every respect except the food.

Drelincourt and I had apparently exhausted all possible conversation after this exchange, so he bowed politely, and I did the same, albeit from a kneeling position, and he took his leave while I returned to my soft fruit gathering.

After a surprisingly long time my bowl was full and I returned to the kitchen to give my bounty to Mechtild. She examined it closely and told me to sit down while she turned out the contents of the bowl on a table top.

'I think you have a generous view of what is ripe, Master,' she said, 'but no matter. A day or so in the warmth here and all will be well. Would you like a glass of ale after your exertions?'

Working in the hot garden had given me quite a thirst, so I gladly accepted and Mechtild brought me a beaker of ale and a crumbly, buttery biscuit. It was delicious. I can taste it even now, over thirty years later. Admittedly I can taste Albrecht's roast mutton too, which made an indelible impression upon me, but not for the same reason.

Mechtild busied herself rolling pastry. 'Are you going away for the summer, Master?'

'No, Mechtild. I have nowhere to go now, since my grandmother died.'

'I thought perhaps you would go to a city somewhere to see the sights.'

This thought had not occurred to me. I would like to see some of the great foreign cathedrals before I die; Chartres, Rouen, Trier, for example. The trouble with foreign cathedrals is that they are all abroad. However, the summer vacation was undoubtedly the best time to make the trip so that I would not have to hurry to get back for teaching. It was probably too late to make plans now, but it was appealing.

'I could give it some thought, Mechtild. What about you?'

'Bless you, Master, I'll be busy here. So long as there are mouths to feed, I'll be in the kitchen, especially with my poor husband being laid up with a broken arm.'

'How is he?'

'Miserable, cantankerous, complaining, overbearing. His normal self, in fact. But we must make allowances for the pain he's in.'

'He is still suffering, then?'

'Well, he says he is, but, begging your pardon, Master, I'm not sure that men know what pain is. They should try having a baby.'

I hear this often from women, and while I do not doubt that there is much truth in it, there is some illogicality in upbraiding men for not having an experience that nature does not allow them to have. Having said that, I have never been present at a birth (except, I suppose, my own, of which I remember absolutely nothing).

I am also bound in fairness to observe that while Albrecht could no doubt merit all the adjectives applied to him by Mechtild, he was always civil to me; but, then, as my grandmother used to say, often after a sideways glance at my grandfather, you never really know someone until you live with them.

I finished the last of my ale and was about to rise from my stool when Mechtild refilled it, so it seemed impolite to refuse and I settled back down.

'If I can do any more to help, Mechtild, please let me know.'

'Bless you, Master, you've done more than most here. Some of the students treat us servants like dirt.'

I was indignant. 'Name names, Mechtild, and I will speak to them severely.'

I meant it. There is no excuse for that kind of behaviour to hard-working staff. You may find this hard to believe, but students are not always as civil as they might be to their lecturers. Only last year I overheard one of them complaining about a "senile old duffer" as they were leaving my lecture, and it is fortunate for that young man that I did not catch whom he was referring to, or I would have told the lecturer in question.

Where was I?

Mechtild patted me on the shoulder as she walked past. 'They're not all like you, Master, more's the pity.'

I was so touched by this encomium that I confess a tear formed in the corner of my eye, which may go some way to explaining why I did not observe the appearance of one of the university porters in the doorway.

'I was told you might be here, Master. The Rector presents his compliments and asks if you will wait upon him at your earliest convenience. Is there something in your eye, Master?'

'No, no — just a summer cold, I think,' I said hurriedly. 'I will wait upon the Rector at once.'

'Very good, Master,' said the porter, remaining exactly where he was.

'I'll just finish this drink,' I added.

'Oh. You don't need me to escort you?'

'No, thank you. I know the way.'

'Very good, Master. If I may say so, sir, I wouldn't keep the Rector waiting. He doesn't seem in a very good mood.'

Drelincourt was a sophisticated and elegant man with a high forehead and a sharp nose. When annoyed he looked like a bird of prey about to sink his talons into you, so I could guess what the porter meant.

'There! All finished. I'll catch you up.' I stood and called my thanks to Mechtild.

'Now, don't you let that Rector be beastly to you, Master!' she scolded.

'I don't think I've done anything to upset him,' I chuckled.

'No, well, you see you don't.'

I ascended the stairs to Drelincourt's study. The door was, as usual, open, so that he could see who was approaching.

'You sent for me, Rector?' I said.

'Yes, I did. I've had a letter.' He held it up as if someone had given him a soiled napkin. 'It's from the Stadhouder.'

Suddenly I did not feel quite so well.

Drelincourt did not offer it to me, by which I understood that it was addressed to him rather than me, but invited me to sit.

'His Excellency sends his compliments to the university and asserts his wholehearted support for our efforts here.'

That was a good start on the face of it. The snag was that I knew that when William wrote like that there was a sting in the tail coming.

'He finds that he has a mission of the most delicate nature which is crucial to the interests of the country and he considers that you are the person best placed to carry it off successfully, Mercurius.'

'I'm really not,' I protested.

'Yes, well, we both know that his statement is unlikely to be literally true, but since we do not know what the mission is, it is hard to assess your chances of success.'

'The Stadhouder doesn't say?'

'No. He only says that it will probably last some months, that he will reimburse the salary of any replacement for you that we have to recruit, plus an enhancement of one-tenth, and that we are not to attempt to contact you during that time.'

'I was rather hoping...' I said falteringly. 'The third volume of my *Commentary*...' Words failed me.

'There may be some time to work on it during your mission,' the Rector said brightly. 'Now, as to practicalities, the Stadhouder says that your presence is not immediately urgent, so you have a couple of days to settle any outstanding debts and say farewell to any loved ones you may have before travelling to The Hague at the weekend. I will lend you my carriage for the journey, if you wish.'

'Thank you, Rector.'

'Do you have any debts, Mercurius?'

'I think I owe three stuivers at Steen's Inn, but otherwise, no,' I replied.

'And any loved ones?'

'No, Rector. I am quite alone in the world.'

I assume that William was hinting at mistresses or something of the sort, but I have never kept one. Such women are expensive to maintain and interfere with a man's work, besides which I am sure that when my grandmother was alive she would have walked the length of the country to clip my ear if she had heard of any such wickedness. However, there was one woman I was dreading having to say goodbye to.

'Well, there you have it, Mercurius. We are to part temporarily while you undertake a mission that, by the sound of it, will involve some peril.'

I had been trying not to think about that. Every mission William had for me seemed to involve some peril; and this matter of settling my affairs certainly had an ominous ring.

The Rector had stood and was extending his hand. 'Mercurius, may God go with you. Your exploits have redounded to the honour of the university and we are proud of you. I hope you will succeed and return to us in triumph once more.' He left unsaid, 'but I doubt it somehow', though I could read it in his face.

I retreated down the stairs in something of a daze. There had been no phrase such as 'if you choose to accept this mission' or 'let me know what you think'. It seemed I was expected to hazard my life once again in the Stadhouder's interest.

In fairness to him, he was a brave man and would think nothing of risking his life for his country. The trouble was that he expected everybody else to think the same way, whereas I wanted no more danger in my life than lifting a heavy book off a high shelf.

I had not planned to go to Steen's Inn until the evening but I thought I had better pay the three stuivers now rather than die in debt. This may seem a gloomy thought, but I recalled that this would be my fifth mission for the Stadhouder. On the first, I was almost stabbed to death in an alleyway. The second saw me kidnapped and threatened with my throat being cut, while on the third I was required to listen to a consort of viols for a whole evening. On the fourth, I was thrown into prison and sentenced to hang. It was no great surprise that I viewed the prospect of more of the Stadhouder's dirty work with no little concern.

As I trudged towards the Langebrug a new plan occurred to me, namely to get blind drunk and stay that way until Saturday so that I would not think about my impending date with doom. On the other hand, a carriage journey after three days of beer would be hellish and I should hate to send the carriage back with the upholstery reeking of regurgitated beer, so I decided to just pay the three stuivers and leave.

Jan Steen had died some years earlier, but to the locals it was still known as Steen's Inn, and the new landlord was no less jovial, so I should not have been surprised that he had automatically poured me a beaker of ale when I entered, and it seemed impolite not to drink it.

'You look troubled, Master,' he said.

'I am. You see a dead man before you.'

'Surely not? You look hale and hearty enough.'

'Nevertheless, I am not long for this world. I have to undertake a perilous journey.'

'Is the university sending you to the Indies?'

'No. I have to go to The Hague.'

Said like that, I can see that the hazard was not immediately apparent, and the landlord clearly felt that there was no more to be said. For that matter, if he had asked me, I could not say much about it, partly because no doubt it was a secret mission and partly because it was a secret even from me.

I drank up, wished him farewell, and walked back to the Academy. How lovely my adopted city of Leiden looked! How fond I was of its little squares, its fine buildings and its stinking canals! Would I ever see it again?

There was no putting it off. I had to say goodbye to Mechtild. I knocked at the kitchen door.

'Master! Is something wrong? You look so sad.'

'I am summoned once more by the Stadhouder.'

'Are you off once more to that England place?'

'I do not know. I know only that I am to be gone some time, possibly months.'

'Months? Oh, my dear Master! You'll miss the best of the strawberries. Now, you sit there while I make you a parcel of little treats.'

Mechtild's favoured way of showing affection was to feed me. Her second option was to clasp me to her bosom, for which I preferred to stand, when at least my nose would be able to breathe. She had hugged me once when I was sitting, and held me so close that I was beginning to suffocate by the time she released her grip. On this occasion both methods were tried, Mechtild giving me a small basket and then clasping me to her. I thought I heard her give a stifled sob, but that might have been me.

'Now, Master,' she said, 'tell that Stadhouder if anything happens to you he'll have to answer to me.'

I believe she would have confronted him too. It would almost have been worth dying to see it.

CHAPTER TWO

On Saturday morning the Rector's carriage stood ready, my trunk attached to the back, and Mechtild's basket where I could keep an eye on it in case some rascal thought to deprive me of my pastries. It would have been good to know where I was going and for how long, though it would not have made any difference to my packing since I own relatively few clothes. As a cleric my wardrobe is always sombre, usually black, and strictly functional.

Normally my trunk is full of books, but on this occasion I had only brought a handful, together with an ample supply of ink and paper. My humour had not been improved by the Rector's request that I tidy my room and leave a copy of my will with him 'just in case' so he could dispose of my possessions in accordance with my wishes 'if the need arises'. 'If the need arises' is just a gentle way of saying 'if you die' but the reality behind it is no less brutal for the soft words. The fact that you are reading these adventures shows that I did not die, but I did not know that then.

Drelincourt had lent me his coachman too, which made for interesting conversation since he was a Frenchman and his Dutch seemed to be confined to terms related to horses and the carriage trade, but at least Drelincourt had explained to him where I was going and how to get there. The road from Leiden to The Hague is quite straight and well maintained, so that I might walk there in a morning. I assumed that the horses would get there quicker than that, and so they would have done if the coachman had followed instructions instead of improvising a route of his own. At any event, around midday I was at the Binnenhof in The Hague supervising the unloading of my trunk and being greeted warmly by the Stadhouder's secretary, Bouwman.

'Master Mercurius! You are welcome. Pray come within and I will order wine and food for you.'

This seemed a friendly invitation, and I was just making to follow when I was intercepted by the coachman, who must have run right round the coach to interpose himself between me and the door. He touched his hat in salute and bowed low, and I realised the blackguard was expecting a gratuity. I dug a coin out of my pouch and gave it to him, whereupon he became very effusive in his thanks and wished me all kinds of good things on my travels. It was only as he put the coin in the band of his hat that I realised that I had given him ten times more than I intended but it seemed churlish to chase after him and ask for it back.

'The Stadhouder is occupied at present,' explained Bouwman.

'Of course, I understand.'

'I doubt that he will be long. He is meeting a Prussian ambassador and he can't stand the man. It may be prudent to leave him to calm down after that meeting before I let him know that you have arrived.'

'I bow to your judgement,' I said.

We sat in easy conversation enjoying a light meal together while in the background we could hear William expressing his opinion on a number of aspects of Prussian foreign policy. The language of diplomacy is, of course, French, a language in which I am rather rusty as I have already observed, but even if I had known the tongue I suspect that William's vocabulary owed rather more to the dockside tavern than the elegant salon.

At length the poor ambassador withdrew and William busied himself with rearranging some of the furniture using his boot. Bouwman suggested that this would be a good time for him to show me a Flemish tapestry newly installed in a distant corridor. We were just on our way out of the door when William opened the door opposite.

'Not so fast, Bouwman!' he boomed. 'Ah, Mercurius! How long have you been lurking there?'

I would have objected to anyone else. I do not lurk. However, I judged that in his present humour arguing with William would be a waste of time. Come to think of it, arguing with William in any humour was a waste of time.

'I have not been here long, Your Excellency,' I replied.

William's temper seemed to dissipate. 'I trust Bouwman has been looking after you.'

'Admirably.'

'Very good. Mercurius, I have a little job, and I think it may be ideally suited to your unusual combination of gifts.'

I was unsure whether 'unusual combination of gifts' was a veiled insult, but it seemed not to be.

'I am at your service, Stadhouder,' I said. I might as well appear willing, even if I was far from being so.

'Excellent, excellent! Well, let us withdraw to the inner chamber and I will explain your mission. You too, Bouwman, but lock this door first so that none can overhear us.'

I refrained from suggesting that when William was in a passion he could be overheard from the courtyard outside.

William invited me to sit, and gave me a goblet of wine without asking whether I wanted it. I did, of course. Although William was not a hedonist, nobody dared to give him anything but the best. He probably thought all wine tasted that way, because he had never tasted the nasty stuff. I sampled some

Greek wine once and it was immediately clear why Greece is not a major force in the wine exporting trade.

'Now, to business,' he began. 'You will recall that four years ago I had cause to send you to Amsterdam, Mercurius, because the city was withholding its taxes. Those ingrates are responsible for nearly a third of the income of the state. I cannot turn a blind eye to such disobedience. They bleat about war being bad for business; well, being invaded and overrun by foreigners is bad for business too. And it is the army that is keeping them safe, but they won't pay for it. I could fail to pay the soldiers, I suppose, and what would happen to law and order in Amsterdam if I did that, do you suppose?'

A rhetorical question, no doubt, but a very pertinent one. Impecunious armed men running around a city is not in anyone's interest, and I am sure that the burghers of Amsterdam would suffer greatly if he followed through on that threat. It surprised me that they were prepared to risk it. I guess that they thought that William would not allow such damage to his own cities, but if so then they did not know William, who was prepared to undergo some pain to make his point.

'I am sure that it would not be in their interest, Stadhouder,' I dutifully replied.

'And you are quite right, Mercurius. I have no doubt there would be a spontaneous display of loyalty to me as there was in The Hague a few years ago.'

I do not think I have ever heard the word spontaneous so egregiously misused, though it is just about possible that the Stadhouder believed it himself. Before he became Stadhouder he was kept from power by a pair of brothers called De Witt. Cornelis was arrested and charged with treason, and his brother Johan, previously top dog in the government, went to visit him in prison. Lo and behold, during his visit there was a 'spontaneous uprising' and a mob killed them both, then went quietly home again. Whether William had foreknowledge I do not know, but he did not prosecute the ringleaders. However, there was nothing to be gained by raising the subject at this juncture.

'Have you ever met Dijkvelt?' William asked.

'Dijkvelt?'

'Everhard van Weede van Dijkvelt.'

'I think not, Stadhouder.' I would have remembered a name like that, I thought.

'Sound fellow. He's been in my service for some time as a diplomat. Anyway, I sent him to Amsterdam to try to reason with those blackguards. Of course, they were terribly nice to him and made all kinds of promises, but they've done nothing about it since. Yes, they fervently want the French King to reconsider the tariffs and prohibitions on Dutch trade, and yes, they want me to do something about it, but nothing that costs any money. The rest of the country is quite prepared to fund a proper army, but it'll be only two-thirds of the size I need unless they produce some cash, Mercurius. Now, Dijkvelt is going back and forth to England at the moment, engaged in some very delicate negotiations on my behalf.'

'With King James?' I blurted out.

'Well … yes and no. The thing is, Mercurius, we already have an ambassador there, Van Citters, whom you've met.'

'I remember him.'

'You see, Van Citters' hands have to be kept clean, so he knows very little of what Dijkvelt is doing. That way if it all goes belly up he can plausibly deny all knowledge. He has introduced Dijkvelt at court, of course, and Dijkvelt has been making some arrangements for the smooth accession of the

Princess Mary when her father dies. But, just in case, he has also been meeting some of the leading men of the country who worry that James may try to install someone else as King after him. A Catholic, that is.'

'Is that possible?'

'Who knows? The English are perfidious enough. And now there are worrying rumours that the Queen is with child.'

That didn't so much put a cat amongst the pigeons as throw in a basketful of them. James had two daughters, and William was married to the elder one. He had refused to help James' illegitimate nephew in an attempt to seize the crown only three years before rather than jeopardise Mary's claim to the throne, and now it might all come to nothing if the baby turned out to be a boy.

'Isn't the King rather old to have a child?'

'He's fifty-four, Mercurius. How old are you?'

I did a quick sum. 'Forty-nine.'

'Well, are you too old to father a child?'

'I have no idea. I've never tried.'

'Anyway, his wife is only twenty-nine. Though they've been married about fourteen years. You'd have thought if she was going to have a child it would have happened by now.'

A great private pain lay behind this statement from the Stadhouder. The Princess Mary had miscarried three times already and now seemed to be unable to conceive. That may have been because she and William now spent so much time apart, since he was very much engaged in putting an army together and Mary, while supportive of her husband, did not want one cluttering up the gardens of their palace.

'We're getting off the point, Mercurius. With Dijkvelt out of the way, I was wondering how we might progress matters with the Amsterdammers. Then I remembered my dear friend Mercurius.'

Here we go, I thought.

'You did such a splendid job getting them to pay up last time. If I send you they know they'll lose in the end, so they might as well cough up with good grace. Same plan as last time, Mercurius. I'll lend you a golden collar, a carriage and a body of horse to escort you, and all you have to do is cajole and threaten the mayors into submission. I leave it to you to decide how much cajoling and how much threatening you do. As luck would have it, three of the four are the same as last time — Geelvinck, Huydecoper and Hudde.'

'What happened to Van Beuningen?' I enquired.

'Got married and went mad. The last I heard, he had lost most of his fortune and was writing strange letters to public figures about the end of the world. He's been replaced by a fellow called Nicolaes Witsen. He's a good type, but very cautious. There's also a strange character called Appelman who is tipped as the rising man and will probably poke his nose in. I don't trust him, Mercurius, and my instincts are normally good on things like this, so neither should you. And don't forget to remind Huydecoper that I still have his book.'

On my previous mission it transpired that Huydecoper kept a book in which he wrote all the bribes he had given and received. By means which still cause me to shudder it had come into William's hands, after which Huydecoper had been much more pliable. As a gentleman William had, of course, returned it, but not before making a copy.

'So that's all you have to do in Amsterdam, Mercurius. Barge in, throw your weight around and get my taxes.'

Is that all? You wouldn't like me to learn to juggle or build a warship or two into the bargain?

'Then, after that,' William added, 'I have another little job for you.'

My heart dropped to my boots. Another little job?

Still, at least I could only be murdered once.

CHAPTER THREE

William sent for some wine. Whatever the other little job was, it was clearly going to take some time to explain. It necessitated our retiring to a pair of chairs by the fireplace where William stretched out his legs, insofar as someone of his reduced stature had legs to stretch, and made himself comfortable.

'This is a particularly delicate task,' he began quietly. 'I've been trying to think who would be best suited to it, because it requires someone especially guarded in his speech and known to be good with confidential material. As I said, Dijkvelt is in England, as is the Heer Van Zuylestein.'

This was a bad sign. Everyone knew that Van Zuylestein was the Stadhouder's number one fixer and wherever he was, something important was going on. I was not, at the time, completely *au fait* with all that was going on in England, but I knew enough to know that when James II of England died his daughter Mary would succeed him, and William was married to her. It was very clear that the Stadhouder had no intention of playing second fiddle to his wife, nor would she expect him to; theirs was a true partnership and each had definite and separate gifts to bring to it.

Nor was I unaware that King James had pursued a very aggressive and largely successful policy of Catholicisation of England; how could anyone in the United Provinces not be aware, when the country was heaving with displaced Englishmen plotting against their King? At first these devout Protestants had come to The Hague, but we had reached the point where they could no longer find lodgings there and were therefore spreading through the country. I have nothing against immigrants, though they could at least attempt to learn our language, but they were exciting James and he had written several times to William asking him to expel some and extradite others, to which William was said to have replied that so long as no Dutch laws had been broken, his conception of liberty was that he was not entitled to arrest them.

'Before I say anything to you, Mercurius, I have to give you a standard warning. My plans are complicated and highly secret. They depend on everyone to whom anything is revealed keeping it to themselves. If anyone murmurs so much as a word about their part in this strategy I would have to have them hanged, if only to concentrate the minds of the others. I hope you understand.'

'I do, Stadhouder,' I said, and I meant it. I've always been good at responding to threats. I do immediately what is asked of me. It's healthier that way.

'I would deeply regret having to execute you. You've always been loyal and dependable, and if it ends badly I want you to know that there won't be anything personal in your execution. It'll be purely statecraft and I won't derive any satisfaction from it.'

'That's very reassuring, Stadhouder.' That bit, I didn't mean. It wasn't really very reassuring at all, but there was no point in antagonising him.

'Let's start from first principles, Mercurius. A man of sense such as yourself doesn't need to be told who the biggest threat to the peace of Europe is.'

'Louis XIV of France,' I obediently replied. I had heard it so many times from William's lips that I did not have to think about that one.

'Absolutely right,' William announced, as if I were the smallest boy in a Latin class and had just successfully chanted *amo*, *amas*, *amat*, and so on. I half expected to be given an apple as a prize. 'He still has designs on this country, Mercurius. He's jealous of our commercial success and is doing all he can to ruin us financially. He has blocked our access to his ports, and slapped tariffs on Dutch imports. I also suspect he may have something to do with the sudden arrival of Algerian pirates in the North Sea. I mean, what else would induce them to come here? They probably didn't even know there was such a thing as the North Sea until somebody told them. You see what I'm up against, Mercurius?'

We had a student around this time whose father was the mayor of his home town and who had distinguished himself in the undergraduate examinations by achieving the lowest set of marks ever recorded by a student of the University of Leiden. Such stupidity was unnatural; he must have applied himself with astonishing diligence to attain it. Nevertheless, like William, he attributed his shortcomings to the fact that everyone was against him. I was exempted from these complaints to some extent because I had given him his highest mark of that miserable set; I have always been tender-hearted [Marginal note: Van der Meer seems to have developed a facial tic causing him to open his eyes wide and let his jaw drop. If it doesn't stop I shall have to recommend a surgeon to him] and I like someone who tries hard, so I had given him some credit for writing his own name in legible handwriting and spelling it very nearly correctly. I have never known anyone else to throw a party on the strength of getting a D.

I digress again.

'It's time to put a stop to Louis' little games once and for all, Mercurius, and this year I intend to do exactly that. I plan to give him such a bloody nose that he'll forget all about invading us or interfering with our trade for the rest of his life.'

What patriotic Dutchman could not wish him every success in those endeavours? We needed a period of peace and tranquillity after thirty years of war. Of course, that was not all William's fault; he had only been Stadhouder for sixteen years and other people had started it.

'Cast your mind back to 1672, Mercurius.'

'The Disaster Year.'

William shuddered at the mere use of the words. It had been an awful experience. Jealous of our great success in trade and our substantial profit from our dealings with our new colonies in the East Indies, France, England, Sweden, Münster and Cologne all declared war on us at the same time. For once, Spain was on our side because the Spanish King did not want Louis to get too big for his boots, but we suffered terribly and it was only William's accession to power and his firm generalship that repelled our enemies. Our admirals fought off the English fleet and then we flooded a large part of our country to slow down the French infantry.

'You'll recall that we had long felt safe from French invasion because the Spanish still held the southern Netherlands,' William said. 'They weren't equipped or sufficient in number to defeat us and had stopped trying, but if the French wanted to get to us they had to have the acquiescence of the Spanish or defeat them in combat, neither of which was very likely. But in 1672 the chief reason that the French were able to advance was that they bypassed the Spanish Netherlands by marching through the western fringe of Germany by invitation of the Bishop of Münster and the Archbishop of Cologne.'

I knew all this, of course. Every Dutchman did, and little children were taught not to trust German bishops at school.

'Well, the tide has turned, Mercurius. I'm not going to sit back and wait to be attacked again. We're going to do to Louis exactly what he did to us. And — this is the sweetest part — we're going to do it exactly the way that he did. Maximilian Henry won't know what has hit him.'

This was a reference to the Archbishop of Cologne, Maximilian Henry of Bavaria, a devious Prince of the Church. He took over as Archbishop of Cologne from his uncle, being ordained priest on his thirtieth birthday, would you believe, although he was actually elected the next Archbishop when he was only twenty-eight and not a priest at all. The Pope was reputed to be unhappy about this, but a large chest of gold pieces arrived in Rome and suddenly the Pope didn't seem too worried about it.

This wolf in bishop's clothing persuaded the Bishop of Münster to join in with his nefarious scheme, promising him a chunk of the eastern provinces of our country in exchange for his co-operation. The Bishop of Münster conveniently died in 1683 and Maximilian Henry contrived to get himself elected in his place. I suppose since he was already Archbishop-Elector of Cologne, Bishop of Hildesheim and Bishop of Liège he thought his credentials as a bishop were well established and one more bishopric would not bring much extra workload, especially since he only wanted the lands and money and did not plan to undertake many of the duties.

Unfortunately for Maximilian Henry, between the Disaster Year and this rigged election there had been a change of Pope, and Innocent XI was very hot on sinecures and people holding multiple offices at the same time, so he refused to confirm Maximilian Henry in the post. Maximilian Henry had not subsequently got round to allowing a new election — after all, it had only been five years and organising these things takes time — so he was still pocketing the income, although he was not technically in the job.

'The beautiful thing, Mercurius, is that now that Maximilian Henry is both Archbishop of Cologne and Bishop of Münster I can get my revenge on both offices by attacking one man,' William announced gleefully.

'You're going to attack Germany?' I gulped.

'No, Mercurius. I'm going to attack France. But I'm going to do it by marching through Germany. There's poetic justice for you! Louis won't expect that.'

I was so nonplussed by this notion that I tried to sip my biscuit and bit into my cup, causing me to slop my wine down my front. I hoped William had not noticed.

'Bouwman, get Mercurius a napkin, will you? You'd better refill his cup too.'

'Thank you, Stadhouder. May I ask why you're telling me this?'

'Because, my dear fellow, you are an important part of this plan. You are going to make it all possible.'

'I am?' I squeaked, in a rather higher pitch of voice than I can normally achieve. I must have been under strain.

'Yes, you, Mercurius. Confidentially, I am gathering my armies at Nijmegen.'

Nijmegen is about four days' march from where we were sitting at that moment. It is almost on the border with Germany. I could understand the need for secrecy, because if the Germans discovered that William's armies were mustering there they would unite to repel him. Under normal circumstances you could never get the many German princes to agree about anything, but they would soon unite against William unless they were given a convincing reason not to do so.

'I've bribed a number of German dukes and princes to turn a blind eye to my march,' William continued. 'Money well spent, and it hasn't actually cost that much because they don't think much of Maximilian Henry either. Some of them were prepared to double-cross him for free. In fact, if I'd realised that, I might have persuaded a few to pay me for the privilege of being allowed to join in.'

William took an enthusiastic swig of wine and waved his arm so extravagantly that the wine flew from his beaker and dampened a tapestry behind him. Bouwman ran to dab it with a cloth. 'The thing is, Mercurius, I have an ace up my sleeve. As Prince of Orange I am also the hereditary Count of Moers.'

This was obviously meant to impress me, but since I had never heard of the place the effect was somewhat diminished.

'It's a little area in the western part of Germany, about two and a half days' march from Nijmegen. And by the terms of a treaty I can keep a Dutch garrison there. Now, in the event of civil unrest, or a clear threat to the security of my government there, I can march as many troops as necessary through Germany to Moers, and nobody can stop me. So you see where this is leading?'

It was very clear to me that if I said no I would look like the biggest fool in Christendom in William's eyes, so I had to find a way of gaining some further understanding. 'You're going to send your army into Germany, pretending that it is going to Moers, but actually it will then go to France?'

'Very nearly, Mercurius. It will actually wait in Moers for a while before advancing on France once reinforcements arrive.'

'And these reinforcements will arrive under the same subterfuge?'

'Yes. The first contingent won't be sufficient to quell the disorder, so the Governor of Moers is going to write to me to ask for more troops to be sent.'

'I see. And who is the Governor of Moers?' I asked.

'You are,' said William. 'Or you will be once the paperwork is signed.'

This time the wine sprayed from my mouth. 'Me?'

'Certainly. I need someone I can trust implicitly and — perhaps more importantly — someone the local people will trust too. Someone who has a keen moral sense. Someone who would never behave improperly. An intelligent, compassionate, honest man. Who will fake a public uprising to give me a pretext to move my troops there. But, of course, it mustn't look fake.'

In my dealings with William I had often been taken by surprise, but this was beyond any previous experience. If he had not been the ruler of our country I could have sent for the lunatic keepers and he would have been in one of those odd jackets in no time. And yet, the more I thought of it, the more I could appreciate its cunning. It would certainly take Louis by surprise, and if the nearby German princes had some foreknowledge they were sure to co-operate because they had no love for Louis either. The one weak spot I could see in the stratagem was that it involved me.

'I'm not actually very good at lying, Stadhouder,' I protested.

'Of course you aren't, Mercurius! You're completely useless at it. But that is what will guarantee its success. Nobody will think for one moment that you are not in earnest when you say that you need troops to quell a potential insurrection. And we'll blame the insurrection on Louis' secret agents, of course, so that's a double win. It can't fail.'

It can if it depends on me, I thought.

'And how am I going to fake an uprising?' I asked.

'You aren't, of course. I'll do the devious stuff. All you have to do is to react to it in exactly the way any sensible governor could react. Try not to hang too many of the ringleaders — it only excites sympathy amongst the masses — but I'm sure that you can pull this off just by being yourself.'

William topped up my cup. I seemed to have absentmindedly swallowed the whole lot in one go somewhere along the line.

'Do you remember Captain Pringle?' he asked.

Indeed I did. Pringle was a Scot who had commanded the troop of horse that accompanied me to Amsterdam on my last little job there. A man who, I am sure, possessed the highest military credentials but who was the last person for any task requiring subtlety.

'Yes, Stadhouder.'

'Excellent. Well, as you know, he went back to England when he was recalled by King Charles, but he is a staunch Protestant and was dismissed from the army by his brother King James. He has returned to my service. Now, James has demanded that I return his six regiments to him, but I can hardly do that. First, I need every man I can get, and second, I have no reason to strengthen James' position, have I?'

There had long been British troops in the United Provinces, and very welcome they had been in guarding us against invasion by anyone except the British. They were there to safeguard our small but very Protestant state against any Catholic aggression, but the treaty that placed them allowed for them to be recalled by their King at any time.

'My plan, Mercurius, is to say that of course all those who wish to serve King James may return with my blessing. We'll then reform whoever remains into new regiments. I doubt if half will go back. Anyway, Pringle will accompany you to Amsterdam and then on to Moers, where he is to be commander of the garrison. And this time he won't have just a troop of horse. I don't intend to pussyfoot around those folks in Amsterdam, Mercurius. You'll have more than one troop of horse behind you this time.'

I was feeling queasy. I am not comfortable in the company of rough fighting men, especially those who don't speak Dutch or Latin. 'How many more, Your Excellency?' I whispered, my voice having failed me.

'Oh, I thought two thousand horse and about twenty thousand in total should do the trick. If the mayors don't cough up the money straightaway go on to Moers and leave the bulk of them in Amsterdam for a while. The effect of having to billet that many men at their city's expense or risk them running amok and helping themselves to food should concentrate the mayors' minds wonderfully.'

No wonder William had told the Rector I may be gone some months. If this went badly I might never return.

'Any questions, Mercurius?'

'This Governorship,' I mumbled feebly, 'is it a permanent position?'

'Good heavens, no! Just until the troops get to France, then I'll send someone else and you can go back to Leiden with a suitable token of my gratitude. I don't mind saying, Mercurius, that when we pull this off I'm going to reward those who made it possible handsomely. You'll never need to work again.'

And if we don't pull it off I'll never work again because I'll be swinging on a gibbet somewhere, if not at the hands of the people of Moers then by order of King Louis. That was what happened to inconvenient governors.

William stood up, so I had to do the same.

'Finish your drink and let's go and have some dinner. All this has given me a good appetite.'

Lucky you, I thought. *Personally, I don't feel much like eating.*

CHAPTER FOUR

Normally William ate sparingly, but I was told that on campaign or when plotting he had a healthy appetite. Despite his asthma he was wonderfully energetic that afternoon and much more communicative than usual.

An added delight was that the Princess Mary was present. I had the highest possible esteem for William's wife. Although she was often caricatured as ignorant because her spelling was poor, she was more competent in Dutch than William was in English, and he thought highly enough of her to appoint her as his Regent when he was out of the country. I had always got on well with her, right back to the days of their betrothal when I had been sent to check that she was well-schooled in the Protestant faith, which she certainly was. While she was a dutiful daughter, and loved her father King James, she knew that her first duty was to support her husband. This conflict between them caused her some grief, but she never flinched.

'You have been gone from us too long, Master Mercurius,' she teased me as I kissed her hand.

'Forgive me, ma'am,' I replied, 'I am not made for court life. And my duties lie elsewhere.'

'Of course they do. I hope that one day we can find you some congenial ones here,' she laughed.

There was the best part of a generation between us, for she was barely twenty-six years old, yet I never thought of her as a daughter-figure. She seemed to me to be more mature than her age would suggest.

We were invited to sit, and I was flattered to be invited to take the seat at her right hand, with William at her left. On his left sat a man called Bentinck, a long-time confidant of William who had, it seemed, recently returned from Germany where he had been conducting unspecified business on the Stadhouder's behalf. I assumed that this was connected with obtaining agreement to William's plan to march his army through Germany, but it was not discussed.

'Do you know, ma'am, why I am summoned here?' I asked Mary.

'Why, Master, I believe you are asking me to be indiscreet!'

'Not at all. I merely wanted to know how much I can share with you.'

Mary laid her fork down gently and turned to face me. 'Do you know the first rule of keeping a secret?' she asked.

'No, ma'am.'

'Do not let it be known that you have a secret to keep.'

I had hoped that I might sow some doubt in Mary's mind that I was the right man for William's task, because the one person who might persuade him to think again was his wife, but Mary clearly did not intend to become involved in such discussions.

'I am afraid my visit here will be short-lived, Your Highness,' I said.

'So I understand. You are bound for Amsterdam, I hear, with Captain Pringle.'

'You are well informed, ma'am.'

Mary acknowledged the compliment with a little dip of the head. 'Pringle is a good man, though a Scotsman,' she said. 'Utterly loyal, and there are so few of my countrymen of whom that can be said, don't you think?'

'It is not my place…'

'Oh, come, Master, I will not be offended. When you were last among my people what opinion did you form of them?'

This was a difficult question. My view may have been unduly influenced by their attempt to kill me. 'They are a complex nation,' I answered guardedly.

'Well, that's true. I do not understand them all myself. But, then, there are differences amongst the Dutch, are there not?'

'That is why I am being sent to Amsterdam. I am to persuade the city authorities there to hand over their taxes in full and without delay.'

'You might like to tell them that the latest news is that there is a squadron of French ships being made ready to head for Amsterdam,' Mary said quietly.

I sat bolt upright in my chair. 'Is there? I didn't know that.'

'No, of course you wouldn't, because it's not true. But those pig-headed self-satisfied fat cats in Amsterdam don't know that.'

'Ma'am, with the greatest respect, I cannot lie to them.'

'Well, I'm sure you know what is best, Master. But it could make the difference between being in Amsterdam for six days or six months.'

Put like that, I could see that it wasn't a lie as such; just wild speculation.

'And I hear congratulations are in order, Master. Or should I say Governor?'

'I'm not sure that it is cause for congratulations, Your Highness. I am utterly unsuited to the role.'

'Come now, Master, I have known you these eleven years and I believe the people of Moers are mightily favoured in your appointment. They will be fairly and honestly governed, I am sure.'

Until I fabricate some kind of grand fracas that requires half the Dutch army to come and sort it out, I thought, but decided to keep that to myself. 'You are too kind, ma'am.'

'I speak as I find, Master. Isn't that the Dutch way?'

There was something in what she said. Dutch people — especially Dutch women — are very forthright. They do not let little things like your feelings curb their tongues. Even with those they love, they may seem brusque. I remember my mother once making herself a new skirt which she wore to visit my grandmother in the days before Oma came to live with us.

'It's too short, the colour doesn't suit you and it draws attention to the size of your arse, but apart from that it's fine,' was Oma's verdict.

I miss my grandmother. How proud she would have been to see me installed as Governor of the County of Moers with a fur mantle and a collar of gold and precious stones. She probably would not have had any more idea than I had where the place was, but I am sure she would have worked it into all her conversations at the next market.

'I almost forgot to tell you, Master, that I recently had a letter from the Bishop of London, who asked me to pass on his compliments.'

'Dr Compton is very kind,' I said, and began thinking furiously. If Compton wanted to pass on his compliments he knew where to find me. And how did he know that Mary would be seeing me? I had not been to The Hague for nearly two years, so why write now with such a message? Unless, of course, it was Mary's way of obliquely telling me that she was in communication with some of those in England who were opponents of her father. Compton had tangled with the King on several occasions and was presently suspended from office by command of the Ecclesiastical Commission. Since the King was Governor of the Church of England, but also a Catholic, James thought it improper to exercise his royal power so he handed it over to the Ecclesiastical Commission, a sort of court presided over by that odious fellow Jeffreys who had hanged and transported so many after Monmouth's rebellion. Needless to say, James may have thought it improper to run the Church, but made sure that the Commission did what he wanted by some back-door route anyway.

For a few minutes Mary turned to converse with William, so I faced right to introduce myself to the man seated there. He turned out to be one of those Englishmen I mentioned earlier, a tall, pale-faced man with a narrow nose. His name, he said, was Henry Sydney, and he was very familiar with our country, having commanded one of the English regiments I wrote about earlier.

'Have you business here, mijnheer?' I asked.

Sydney gave a thin-lipped smile. 'Not of a commercial kind. Say, rather, that I am renewing acquaintances.'

This could be a coded reference to all those dissidents who had come here. Perhaps Sydney was keeping them informed of events in England. On the other hand, he might be here to find out what they were up to on behalf of King James. It was all very confusing. It seemed safest to say nothing at all about any controversial subject, so we ate in silence for some time. Sydney finally remarked that we had not seen much rain for the time of year, which seems to fascinate the English. They can talk about rain for hours. Since I could not think of any way that my views on meteorology could be held against me, I decided to agree with his statement. That brought the discussion to an abrupt close.

Mary turned to me again. 'Before you leave, Master, I should be grateful if you could find time to take your leave of me in a more private setting. I have somewhat to say,' she said in a low voice.

[No, Van der Meer, that is not what she was getting at. And stop licking your lips.]

When dinner ended William went to abuse some other ambassador, and I was taken to meet Captain Pringle once again. He was standing in a yard as horses were paraded past him for his inspection.

'I trust I do not disturb you,' I said.

Pringle turned to look at me, an exercise that required a half-pirouette since he had only one eye. A blue velvet eye-patch covered the other. 'Master Mercurius. It is a delight to see you again.'

This was said in a tone of voice that conveyed absolutely no excitement whatsoever.

'As it is for me, Captain; though I regret that it is necessary to repeat our tax-collecting exercise in Amsterdam.'

'Aye, well, if you'd let me hang one of the mayors last time we wouldn't be having this trouble this time. An excess of mercy is never politic.'

Pringle had fashioned an idea that we might more readily speed the mayors' compliance by hanging one from the yardarm of a large ship. I had demurred though I could see his point.

'I will, of course, submit to your orders, as a good military man must, but I hope you will be willing to receive sound advice,' he continued.

His conception of "sound advice" always seemed to involve hanging, flogging or branding someone. Despite this, his men idolised him, telling me proudly that they may have been the scum of the earth, but they were Pringle's scum, which made them superior to any other form of scum.

'Since we are engaged in part on military matters it would be foolish not to seek your opinion,' I replied. This was not idle flattery. I know absolutely nothing of warlike preparations and the horrible thought was beginning to dawn on me that if the French got wind of William's plan they might pre-emptively invade Moers, in which event I would be as much use as a woollen shield.

'Let us first deal with those blackguards in Amsterdam before we turn our minds to such considerations. We cannot dilly-dally as we did last time. The campaigning season is short and the Stadhouder will be keen to move his troops to Moers within the month. We cannot spare more than three or four days in Amsterdam.'

This had not been pointed out to me before. I know that it is considered bad form to hunt certain animals outside particular seasons of the year, so as to spare their young, but I did not know that there was a closed season for warfare. I had no idea what happened on, say, the first day of October, when everyone presumably put a marker on the ground and went home so that they could come back and start killing one another again in the following April.

'I am as keen as you are to resolve this expeditiously,' I said.

Pringle returned to his horse inspection. 'Good. Then we understand each other, Master.'

CHAPTER FIVE

My chamber was very comfortable, with an abundance of cushions and a chair so well-made for study that I briefly contemplated hiding it in my luggage. Readers who have perused previous volumes of my memoirs may recall that on the last occasion that I was in Amsterdam I was given the services of a manservant who turned out to be a disguised lieutenant in the army, and who caused me considerable embarrassment with his cavalier attitude towards serving maids. Honestly, at times I wonder where these throwbacks to the Dark Ages come from. Did they not realise that this was the seventeenth century? [Yes, Van der Meer, I know it is now the eighteenth, but the events I am relating took place in the last century. Do try to keep up.]

I was sure that whatever servant was allocated to me this time would be equally disreputable, and I was determined to set off on the right foot by laying down the law, so when there came a knock on my door around supper time and a young man entered and introduced himself I was fully prepared for any skulduggery he might be contemplating.

'I am Jakob Biesma, Your Excellency. I am to serve you on your journey and remain with you in Moers.'

'Indeed, Biesma? Well, let me get one thing straight from the outset. There is to be no improper behaviour with young women. No drunkenness, and certainly no theft. Is that clear?' I said severely.

Biesma was evidently shocked by my prohibitions, but meekly bowed his head, at which point I caught a glimpse of his tonsure.

'You're a monk?'

'I was, Master. My monastery has recently closed and I entered the service of the Stadhouder as a clerk. He asked for volunteers to go to Moers and since I have no family ties and no home except such as His Excellency directs I stepped forward. I hope that you have no objection to a Catholic secretary?'

'Secretary?'

'Indeed, Your Excellency. You will need a secretary to attend to your papers in Moers.'

'Won't there already be one from the previous Governor?'

'Ah. Your Excellency has not been fully informed.'

'Can we stop all this "Your Excellency" nonsense? Just call me Mercurius.'

'Forgive me, that would be most improper, Your Excellency.'

'Then call me Master.'

Biesma weighed this proposition for a few seconds. 'As you direct, Master. I must explain that the previous Governor and his secretary have been posted to the East Indies.'

Given the prevalence of disease there, this was tantamount to a death sentence.

'Did they displease the Stadhouder in some way?'

'The facts are not known to me, Master, but I understand there were some irregularities in their accounting for taxes.'

That would do it. William would forgive many things, but not handing over taxes in full was not one of them. As to a Catholic secretary, I could see some advantages. The state religion of Moers would, no doubt, be the Reformed Church as in the United Provinces, but in that part of Germany there are a great many Catholics. Maintaining a balance — a (nominally) Reformed governor and a Catholic secretary —

could be an excellent approach to maintaining public confidence. Alternatively, it might just ensure that everyone had someone to complain about.

The concern that I felt around Biesma's presence was that he would be with me most of the day, and there is nobody more likely to detect a closet Catholic than another Catholic. It says much for William's toleration that he chose the best man for the job, regardless of their religion. Throughout his career he was surrounded and guided by people of both Protestant and Catholic belief, and he made no distinction. Indeed, I believe that William would have appointed a Hindu so long as he was opposed to Louis XIV.

Since everyone seemed to know something about my mission that had been withheld from me, it seemed to do no harm to ask if there was anything more I should hear. 'Is there anything else I don't know, Biesma?' I enquired.

'I don't know, Master. I don't know what you don't know.'

'Let's approach this another way. Why don't you tell me everything you know about our mission, just to see if I lack any useful information?'

Biesma nodded his agreement, then stood for some moments in silence, his eyes flicking from side to side as he mustered his thoughts. 'We are to go first to Amsterdam where you have business that I am told need not concern me.'

That was a promising start.

'We are then to go to Nijmegen, where the Stadhouder is collecting his armies. We will meet the senior officers there and make a list of their needs so that we can ensure that all is ready for them when they arrive at Moers.'

'And how are we to achieve that in so short a time?' I asked, dreading the answer.

'As Governor, you will issue decrees confiscating all that is needed for the war effort. I am to make a list of those entitled to compensation which the Stadhouder will assure.'

The reader will forgive any scepticism I might feel on this point. William was a fair man, and I could imagine him being very willing to pay for what he took. On the other hand, money is money and William never had enough of it. Armies are expensive, and William never thought he had enough of them either.

Herein lies his principal dilemma. He always needed more soldiers, and therefore he always needed more money. The irony is that some of his greatest victories were won with inferior forces, because he saw to it that his troops were well trained and well equipped; which, of course, required more money.

'Was there anything else?'

'Once arrived in Moers, you are to eradicate the corruption of the previous administration.'

'Do we have any indication what form this corruption may have taken?'

'I don't, Master. Do you?'

'Not a word. We shall have to see when we get there.'

'We are to collect together the supplies required by the army during their short stay in Moers on their way to their secret location.'

'Which is?'

'I don't know,' said Biesma, adding quite reasonably, 'it's a secret.'

'It's not a secret from me, but I'll tell you later.'

Biesma accepted this as entirely appropriate. 'I think that is all, Master.'

The word "all" was being severely stretched there. Basically, we had to twist a lot of mayors' arms, given three days to do it, or leave my escort there until they paid up, then go on to Nijmegen and meet up with an army before racing to Moers to hurriedly collect together the supplies the army would need, by any means necessary, on the promise that the Stadhouder would eventually pay for them. Then, and only then, could I take up my duties as Governor of Moers, but at least that posting would draw to an end once the troops reached France. Presumably, since Moers was a county near the front line of a war, I would be replaced by a military governor, perhaps even Pringle. If it meant I could get back to Leiden quicker I did not mind losing my escort. I am not worth robbing anyway.

Biesma withdrew, and I decided to go to bed early. I had just made myself comfortable when someone came to hammer on my door to tell me that evening prayers would be in ten minutes.

I clambered out of bed and dressed again. The things I do for religion.

There was no gainsaying it. Pringle in full dress uniform was a magnificent sight.

He had acquired a new orange sash and was wearing a short cape of blue lined with orange silk. His hat bore a fine white feather and all the metalwork about his person shone brightly. The only drawback was that he was exhibiting this in my room at half-past five in the morning.

'We will be ready to go in half an hour, Governor,' he announced.

'You may be. I won't,' I muttered.

'I never thought you addicted to sloth,' he replied.

'It's not that,' I said, not entirely truthfully. 'I am under orders not to depart without taking my leave of the Princess Mary.'

'Is that all?' said Pringle. 'Why not go and see her?'

'She'll be in her bedchamber,' I pointed out.

'Indeed she will. It's the one time of day when we know exactly where to find her.'

'What do you think the Stadhouder would conclude if he discovered that I had been in his wife's bedroom alone when she was in her bedclothes?'

'You won't be alone,' said Pringle. 'I'll come with you. And she's always surrounded by a bunch of her ladies anyway. The only time she's alone in her bedchamber is when William dismisses her ladies because he fancies a bit…'

'Yes, I get your drift,' I interrupted hurriedly. 'Nevertheless, it seems highly improper to me.'

'The sooner we get to Amsterdam, the sooner we leave,' Pringle replied. 'And the more time you'll have to make the necessary arrangements at Moers.'

I could not argue with that. Some compromise was necessary, but I was not going to have my movements dictated by an army officer. I was, after all, to be the Governor of Moers, so I intended to act like one.

'We will leave in an hour. I will dress and shave now. Meanwhile, I should be grateful if you would arrange for someone to inform the Princess's ladies that I intend to take my leave of her very soon.'

Pringle saluted, turned on his heels, and clanked off down the hall. Having undertaken to prepare myself, I rolled out of bed and was doing exactly that when Biesma knocked. He looked disgustingly fresh and alert.

'All is ready, Governor. I will send two men for your travelling chest. I am to conduct you to mijnheer Bouwman, who has various things that you will need. And I am to tell you that the Princess Mary will meet you in her chamber before you go.'

'Thank you, Biesma,' I said. 'You are very diligent.'

What I really wanted to say, of course, was that he was an infernal nuisance who could boil his head, because after many months of starting work at seven o'clock I had been looking forward to a lie-in. I clearly needed to manage expectations around this.

'Biesma,' I said, 'I wish to make it clear that when we get to Moers I will have no appointments before eight o'clock; nine o'clock on a Saturday. Is that understood?'

'As you wish, Governor.'

'Very good. My chest is packed. You may arrange its collection.'

'Begging your pardon, Governor, but it may be convenient to take it to Secretary Bouwman's room first. The items you are to take are quite substantial and valuable.'

'Yes, well, that is what I meant.'

'Very good, Governor.'

I caught a glimpse of myself in a looking-glass. I did not like what I saw there. I was turning into the kind of person I had never wanted to be. I decided there and then that I must fight against the corrupting influence of power, and I resolved that as a superior I would resolutely maintain Christian qualities, a promise that I believe I have kept in the succeeding thirty-four years. [Marginal note: Van der Meer's cough is troubling him once more. I have recommended the juice of a pound of rhubarb every day. It won't cure him but given what rhubarb does to one's bowels, he won't dare to cough again.]

Bouwman was up and about, another of those people who go around spreading untoward cheerfulness in the morning. I tried to match his disposition, because he was a good man.

'Good morning, Master — I beg your pardon, Governor,' he corrected himself.

'Good morning, Master Secretary,' I replied, since we were being formal.

'I have laid out some items here on the table,' Bouwman continued. 'Here is your gold chain of office, with seven sapphires, three rubies and three emeralds.'

'Are they real?' I gasped.

'Certainly not. The real ones were sold some time ago. But they are convincing counterfeits, don't you agree? The gold, however, is genuine, and His Excellency requires me to ask you to sign for this. Within your baggage train is a nondescript cart in which fifty thousand guilders are concealed to meet your expenses on your mission and to achieve the supply of the army when in Moers. Only Pringle knows that it is there.'

A quick sum told me that was just two and a half guilders per man, so I hoped that they were used to a frugal life.

'And there is your sword of office.'

'Forgive me, I am a clergyman. I cannot in good conscience wear a sword.'

'Your scruples do you credit, Governor. However, permit me to point out that it is an antique sword and would probably fall apart if you attempted to use it in anger. It is not worn but carried in front of you on formal occasions.'

'Ah, that makes a difference.'

'The regalia that you will carry is this baton.' He indicated a stick with a knob on each end. It was black and the knobs appeared to be gold. I tried picking it up. It was remarkably heavy. 'It is ebony and gold, Governor. Please try not to drop it. It is doubtful that it could be repaired in Moers.'

'I'll bear that in mind.'

'Now, here are your letters of commission. This one empowers you to conduct the negotiations in Amsterdam. You will see that it allows any settlement at your discretion so long as the taxes are paid in full and at once.'

I had to take his word for that since the document was sealed.

'Then this is your letter of appointment as Governor of Moers, which is to be publicly displayed. The third document describes your emoluments, the expenses that will be reimbursed, and instructions for the submission of claims in respect of them. It is best if that one is kept private.'

The salary is that small, eh? I thought. (Actually, I was wrong about that. The salary was far in excess of anything I might ever have hoped to earn at the university. It was a shame that it was only going to last a couple of months and that I would have to do such disagreeable things to earn it; but then, perhaps that was why the salary had to be so high.)

'It remains only for me to wish you success and Godspeed you, Governor. I shall, of course, pray for your safety.'

I thanked him whilst becoming rather agitated that my safety needed praying for. To my way of thinking, being a Governor meant sitting in a large hall much of the day giving orders while surrounded by soldiers. What danger could befall me?

CHAPTER SIX

I found my way to the Princess's chamber. At my knock one of her ladies opened the door slightly, curtseyed politely, then looked behind her to check that all were decent.

The reader will understand that I have very little experience of ladies' chambers, and therefore I cannot compare what I saw with other examples; nor, perhaps, are my descriptive powers adequate to explain what I saw. There were devices on dressing tables, the purposes of which eluded me [No, Van der Meer, I know what a dressing table is for; I was talking about the objects on them] and I would not have thought it possible for so many young women to occupy a room simultaneously. Mary sat in a long boudoir coat as various attending ladies sculpted her hair, applied cosmetics and bedecked her with jewellery. I had no idea that women had to do such things in order to have breakfast. Perhaps I should say ladies rather than women; I had seen my mother and grandmother settle for a good wash and a quick brush of their hair before starting their day.

Mary greeted me cordially and asked her ladies to pause in their work.

'Please leave us,' she commanded. It was a tone of voice I had never heard her use. This was a serious Mary, not the playful young woman I had come to know.

'But, Your Highness…' one stammered.

'I think Master Mercurius is not a man to take liberties with a married woman,' she barked. 'My reputation is perfectly safe.'

The women reluctantly filed through a door into an adjoining room.

'I am grateful to you for taking your leave in this way,' she began.

'I was honoured to receive your direction,' I replied.

'I do not direct you in anything, Master. I advise, and that is all. But I wanted to say that my husband and I are sensible that we are asking a great deal of you in this mission. Please be assured that what you are doing is vital to our chances of success in our undertaking, else we would not dare to ask. And we are certain that you are the best man for this job.'

Was that a royal "we" or was she speaking for William too?

'I know that you are not a man who prizes luxury or expects to have attendants dance around him. This experience will be mortifying for one of your simple tastes. But I know that your head will not be turned. It would be easy, Master, to view Moers as just a tool to be used in a greater cause, but the people there are our subjects and they deserve good government. I know that you will do your utmost to secure that for them.'

She opened a drawer and produced two parcels, one very small and the other rather larger. 'I wanted to give you a small parting gift. Only God knows if we shall see each other again.'

Those creepy feelings that Bouwman had induced reappeared. First I am told that my task may be dangerous and then that there is a risk that I may not return. I could find no words apart from a rather embarrassing gulp.

Mary pressed the larger parcel into my hand. It was a book wrapped in a simple green cloth tied with a matching ribbon. 'You may open it if you wish.'

I carefully did so. It was a copy of a book by Machiavelli entitled *The Prince.*

'I do not recommend all the stratagems described here, Master. Some are beneath you. But it is always good to know of them so that one can tell if they are being practised on one.'

I wondered briefly whether she was speaking from experience. She certainly was no fool when it came to politics and government. 'Thank you, Your Highness. This generosity is unexpected. I do not know what to say.'

No sooner had I said it than I realised that my comment might have been interpreted to mean that the Princess was normally close-fisted and I regretted the remark, but she seemed not to notice.

Without a word she handed me the small parcel, a tiny box, quite plain, but with the letter M on the lid. I opened it to find a gold ring. There was no stone, but the centre was flattened to give a square on which there was some kind of image that I could not quite make out.

'You have it upside-down, Master,' Mary explained.

I inverted it and could see that the device was the letter M with a crown above it.

'My uncle King Charles gave it to me when I left England to marry William. He said that some day I would be Queen. When that happened, he must be dead, but he wished to give me a gift against so propitious a day. It seems that day will not come. My sister Anne writes to tell me that my stepmother is big with child, who will be King James' heir. But I must put this ring to good use, and if you stamp a letter's seal with this ring I will know that it is from you and for my eyes only. You must promise to tell me only the truth in such letters, Master.'

'I am staggered, ma'am. Surely this is too personal an item to part with?'

'Tut-tut, Master, let us be practical. If the child is a boy it will supersede me in the succession to the throne. And we must wish for my stepmother the safe delivery of a healthy child; to do otherwise would be unchristian, surely?'

I bowed. This was a magnificent and noble woman. 'I will use it as you direct.'

'Advise, Master. A man may direct, but a woman only advises.'

I am not sure that there was any real distinction being advice and direction where Mary was concerned. Her advice sounded like an instruction to me, but one I was always willing to take.

She stood and extended her hand. I went to kiss it but she wanted me only to hold it.

'Master, I pray that whatever befall you will not think ill of us. We do what we do for the good of our countries.'

'I have never doubted that, Your Highness.'

I was rather puzzled by her comment, because I could not think of any circumstances in which I would think ill of her. Her husband was a rather different matter, but William was at least utterly consistent. He was always completely ruthless and indifferent to the wishes of others, but there was nothing personal in it. The only person he hated was Louis XIV, and I believe he would have spoken well of Satan himself if the Lord of Darkness had taken against Louis. No danger of that, by the way; Louis and Satan were best friends, at least according to William.

'I hope to see you again before too long, Master, but only God knows where or when. Farewell, and go in peace.'

And she kissed me. She actually kissed me. On the cheek — well, on the side of my eye, really, because she was a tall woman. She was, I think, the first woman outside my family to do so, and I was still in a daze when Bouwman led me to the courtyard where my carriage awaited, accompanied by a troop of men on horseback in blue uniforms which, while splendid, were unsuited to the battlefield.

'Captain Pringle,' I said, 'I am not particularly skilled in mathematics but this doesn't look like two thousand men to me.'

'They aren't all here, Governor. This is your personal escort. The others have set out along the road to Amsterdam under the command of Lieutenant Schoenmaker. Soldiers move slower than carriages, you see, so they departed last night.'

'Ah, very good.'

Pringle seemed to be waiting for something. After an awkward few seconds he explained. 'You need to get in the carriage, Governor, unless you intend to run alongside.'

'Ah, indeed.'

I did just that.

'If you need anything during your journey, Governor, just rap on the rear of the carriage. Your valet, Tap, is riding there and will attend to your needs.'

'Shouldn't I be introduced to him?'

'Why? He's a servant. Are you going to ask to be introduced to all your servants?' Pringle lowered his voice. 'Men of rank ignore servants, Governor. You must learn to do the same or you'll give the game away.'

What game? I thought. *I am a genuine Governor. I have a letter that says so. And I intend to govern the county of Moers to the best of my ability. If we ever get there, that is.*

The journey to Amsterdam was every bit as tedious as I remembered from the previous time. The United Provinces form a small country and if the weather stayed fair we might arrive by nightfall, though this would be a long walk for the horses.

A horrible thought occurred to me. 'Pringle, I hope we are not stopping at Leiden for lunch again?'

That had been an excruciating experience last time. The Rector of that year and I had felt equally uncomfortable about the whole thing.

'No, we'll be too early for that, but we'll feed and water the horses. Maybe you can suggest somewhere for my men to refresh themselves.'

I had no intention of mentioning Steen's Inn. Not only would they not all fit in, the thought of what thirsty soldiers might do to my favourite hostelry did not bear thinking about. Fortunately, I could tell them to keep to the right as they entered Leiden and follow the water to the Botermarkt, where they could disperse to enjoy a number of inns.

Pringle formed the men up and addressed them in a voice loud enough to be heard as far off as the university. 'Remember, men, whose men you are and whose uniform you wear. Come back drunk, and you'll be lashed till your back's raw. Steal, and it'll cost you your hand. Molest a woman, and it'll cost you more than your hand. Is that clear?'

There was a chorus of 'Aye, sir!'

'One hour, then. Dismissed!'

They scattered, leaving Pringle, myself and a third individual whom I did not know.

'This is Tap,' Pringle explained.

'I'm pleased to meet you, Tap,' I said. 'What is your name?'

'Tap, sir.'

'Your Christian name.'

'Oh — Henk. Hendrik. But usually Henk.'

'Very good, Henk.'

Pringle tugged at my sleeve.

'He's a servant, normally to be addressed by his surname.'

'He's a personal servant, and therefore more intimate.'

Pringle rolled his eyes as if I were a lost cause, but I felt that I had made my point.

'Now, Tap, where are you going to lunch?'

'Wherever you do, sir. Not at your table, of course. But I'll serve you and then grab something myself.'

'Do you have money?'

'No, sir.'

I gave him a coin.

'Captain Pringle and I have some private business. I won't need you for an hour. Get yourself some refreshment.'

He bowed slightly and ran off.

'What private business was that?' Pringle enquired.

'We'll think of something. But for all I know he may be a spy.'

'Of course he is,' Pringle replied. 'I picked him myself.'

CHAPTER SEVEN

For those of my readers who have never seen Amsterdam, let me explain that it is basically Gomorrah but with better architecture.

A brief stroll around the areas fronting the docks — and almost everywhere in Amsterdam is not far from a dock — will introduce you to every type of human depravity and sinfulness you have ever thought of and several which will not have crossed your mind. Women of easy virtue abound and display themselves with impunity at doors and windows, thievery is rampant and fights are commonplace.

I am not sure what the authorities do about these things, but the church relies on bloodcurdling sermons from the pulpit each week. By my reckoning there must have been at least a couple of hundred of these in each church since I was last there, and they appeared to have had no effect at all.

We had stayed at an inn just outside Amsterdam overnight so that I could arrive fresh in the morning and get straight to work. On my previous visit I had been billeted on one of the mayors, Johannes Hudde, who had proved a hospitable man, and he swiftly offered to put me up again. I thanked him and then said in my sternest voice that I had not planned to spend long in Amsterdam, having important business for the Stadhouder elsewhere, and would therefore be content with a room in an inn. As I expected, Hudde clearly took that as a very bad sign and exchanged meaningful glances with the other mayors — for Amsterdam had four.

The one I expected most trouble from was Johann Huydecoper, whose book listing bribes given and received had been appropriated by my servant, copied by the Stadhouder's staff, and then returned with a warning that failing to see things our way would result in the publication of the book. It was not that the merchants of Amsterdam would be shocked by the giving and receiving of bribes, because they were all at it themselves anyway, but that some would be shocked to discover how much others had been paid for lesser services.

Huydecoper began by questioning why William was so intent on war with France, when we were much more likely to gain what we wanted by diplomatic negotiation. I paused before answering, largely because I did not have an answer until, by some good fortune, Mary's words came back to me.

'And how will you negotiate with the French squadron which, intelligence has it, is headed this way to blockade our ports?'

'What squadron?' Huydecoper asked. 'Has anyone seen this mythical squadron?'

That was a rather unpleasant jolt to my self-satisfaction at having remembered my lines, and I was wondering how to respond when Witsen spoke up.

'There are reports this morning that such a squadron has been encountered close to Dunkirk.' He spoke quietly, yet with some authority.

'And you credit these reports?' Huydecoper snapped.

'I neither credit nor discredit them. I report that there are reports, that is all.'

'And who gives out these reports?'

'The Master of the *Black Lion*, a vessel of around two hundred tons, lately returned from Lisbon.'

'And you have spoken to him personally?'

'No,' Witsen replied. 'But he spoke to my agent this morning. He does not want to cause general alarm but suggests that valuable cargoes might best be carried in convoy.'

Huydecoper seemed to have calmed down a little. 'That would be inconvenient.'

Geelvinck chipped in. 'This on top of the Barbary pirates!'

'What Barbary pirates exactly?' Huydecoper demanded to know.

'They seem to be active again. Whipped up by France, no doubt. Why do your own dirty work when you can set someone else to do it for you?' I said.

These pirates had never gone away, but their activity depended to some extent on conditions at home in North Africa. Usually they cruised the Middle Sea looking for Europeans to enslave, but about sixty years before they had raided as far as Iceland, and since then had been seen in Ireland, England and our own coasts. I was on safer ground in referring to them, because they reappeared at intervals, particularly when France and the Italian states exerted themselves to clear the Mediterranean. Whether Louis had suggested that they raid our waters, or whether it was a consequence of his driving them away from his own south coast, was a moot point. Either way, they were a confounded nuisance to the traders of Amsterdam, and therefore a considerable help to me.

Sensing that Geelvinck, Witsen and Hudde seemed to be sympathetic to William's demands, it seemed prudent to let them have a try at persuading Huydecoper.

'If you will excuse us,' I said, 'Captain Pringle and I must make some arrangements for my brief stay in Amsterdam. It should not take more than an hour, so I shall leave you to discuss the Stadhouder's demands and return very soon.'

I bowed and swept out of the room, the majesty of the action being somewhat marred by my gown snagging on a door handle, and descended to the street.

'That was very well done,' Pringle remarked out of the corner of his mouth. 'That should give them pause for thought.'

'It was very convenient that those reports reached Amsterdam when they did,' I replied. 'It has made our task rather easier, I fancy.'

Pringle said nothing, but gazed fixedly ahead. His silence discomfited me.

'Just a moment,' I said. 'That wasn't coincidental, was it?'

'How do you mean, Governor?'

'It's just too convenient. What don't I know?'

'It was for your own good, Governor. If you had known you would not have been so convincing.'

'If I had known what?'

Pringle sighed and reluctantly explained. 'When we stopped for the night, Tap and a couple of my officers continued into the city. They headed for the docks, on the lookout for a ship newly arrived whose master could be induced to speak freely about a French squadron. Fifty guilders well spent if you ask me.'

'Fifty guilders!'

'When you think of the sum the Stadhouder will receive, he won't begrudge us those fifty guilders. And the master won't get all the money. He has to bribe his first mate and one or two sailors to make the story convincing.'

He may have been sure that William would reimburse us. I wasn't. He might give us thirty, if we were lucky.

'Why would the master do that?'

'Well, because he has been paid well to do so.'

'But it is a lie!'

'Yes, but a very lucrative one. And look at it this way, Governor. We don't know that it's a lie. There may well be a French squadron heading our way. We just can't prove that it's true. But it doesn't matter to the master. If a squadron appears he can bask in having been the first to encounter it. If it doesn't he can say that his raising the alarm frightened them off. Either way he gains money and fame, and what more does any man want?'

'How about a clear conscience?'

'That is a luxury many men cannot afford, Governor.'

'How cynical! Better to be poor than to be dishonest.'

'That's easy for you to say. You're not poor. And those religious men who have taken vows of poverty are voluntarily poor. They can stop being poor if they want. Besides which, they know where their next dinner is coming from, so their poverty is irrelevant.'

'Nevertheless, the mayors are about to make an important decision based on spurious information. It is my clear duty to put them right.'

I marched resolutely towards the door to City Hall only to have it held shut by a long arm in a blue velvet glove.

'Not so hasty, Governor. The decision they are about to make is the very aim of your visit here. The sooner they reach it the quicker you can move on.'

'Good policy cannot be based on my personal self-interest,' I objected.

'Of course not. Perish the thought. However, let us consider an alternative line of thought. Suppose that we had arrived this morning to find that the mayors had convened last evening and decided to pay the taxes. What then?'

'I'd have been delighted, accepted gleefully, and left them in peace.'

'Yet you would have had no idea how they reached that decision. It might have been based on faulty information.'

'Well, obviously. But not *my* faulty information.'

'Does it matter where the information comes from?'

'It does if I am implicated in a falsehood.'

'But, I repeat, you don't know it's false. It's plausible because these men, famed for their sagacity, believe that it could be true. The French have ships, and those ships have to be somewhere. They might as well be in the North Sea as anywhere else.'

'I suppose…' I said uncertainly.

'Not that French ships are anything to worry about,' Pringle sniffed. 'The French don't have a reputation as shipbuilders.'

'They don't?'

'Not at all. When Kings want ships built well, they send for Dutchmen to do it. Consider the King of Sweden; when he was planning the mighty *Vasa* he had it built by Dutchmen.'

'The *Vasa* keeled over and sank within a mile of its launch.'

'Indeed. But it was beautifully constructed. It was the plans that were faulty, not the workmanship. We lead the world in building fast ships.'

I noticed that Pringle had awarded himself Dutch citizenship in that sentence.

I had to admit that there was some truth in Pringle's analysis. Despite my misgivings, the decision was for the mayors to make, and it was not my business how they reached it. And even if an untruth were offered, they were under no compulsion to accept it.

I allowed Pringle to lead me away to the inn that he had nominated as my lodgings. It was called the Waterside Inn, which would not have been unusual in Amsterdam except that this particular hostelry was not on the water's edge. To be fair, it once had been, but as a result of the aggressive reclamation of land it was now quite a distance from any substantial body of water, a fact that the owners obstinately refused to recognise. Amsterdammers can be like that, as I was discovering.

My chamber was not large, but at least I had one. The majority of those staying there were accommodated in a single large room.

'Where will you stay?' I asked Pringle.

'My place is with my men. I can sleep anywhere,' he claimed. 'Soldiers have to.'

'And where will they sleep?'

'In the big church down the road.'

'The Nieuwekerk? Won't that be inconvenient for the locals?'

'I do hope so. That's why we're doing it. The more tiresome it is to have us around, the quicker they'll give in to get us to move on. I may stable a few horses there too.'

In the event, my stay in Amsterdam was mercifully brief. When we returned to the City Hall we were greeted by the mayors who said that, after due consideration, taking one thing with another, looking at the matter from both sides, they had decided, not without some reservations, that it was their duty to make the tax payments that William wanted. They did, however, want assurances that the money would not be devoted entirely to the army, but that the navy should receive sufficient to ensure that Dutch sailors were not at undue risk from French ships and Algerian pirates.

'I am not authorised to give assurances of the kind you seek, but I shall include your request in my report,' I said. 'It seems very reasonable to me.'

At that point I thought my misery was over, but Huydecoper stepped forward to invite me to an evening of lute music at his house. There was also to be an eminent Italian singer who would perform a few songs. Despite my detestation of lute music I accepted and tried to look keen about it, notwithstanding my experiences on a previous similar occasion when the villain masquerading as my manservant stole Huydecoper's book. I resolved that this time I would attend alone.

I was greeted on arrival by Huydecoper and his wife. Pringle bowed so low to her that I feared his breeches might split up the back. I was not aware that the invitation had been extended to him, too, but he explained that he was my bodyguard, the Stadhouder having heard about the lack of law and order in some parts of Amsterdam. As you might imagine, that did not go down well with my host, who turned a curious shade of purple for a few minutes, but Pringle followed it with another sweeping bow and 'Your servant, sir,' as if this excused any and all rudeness on his part, before pushing his way into the salon and finding a goblet of wine. I eventually managed to catch up with him.

'If you're my bodyguard, shouldn't you stay with me?' I hissed.

'Ah, that is what an enemy would expect me to do. I go before you to sniff out danger in your path. Have some of these oysters, they're really rather good.'

'Try not to upset anyone, Captain. They could yet change their minds.'

'Aye, they could. But I have a document in my pocket that would brand them turncoats if they did. Relax, Governor; with good fortune you'll never have to see these people again.'

'I thought that the last time.'

I would gladly have never seen the lutenist again. He had an annoying habit of flicking his head back while he was playing to make his hair swing freely. This elicited a number of female gasps from the audience, because women are generally besotted with lute players, at least until one attempts to court their daughters. When I say "court" I mean something altogether more animalistic that we need not specify here.

I also noticed that upon playing the last chord of a piece he flung his arm upwards in an arc and struck an heroic pose which he held until the applause was under way. I contrived always to have my hands full at that point since I should have felt a hypocrite if I had given him any encouragement; not that he needed any, playing no less than four encores although the applause was sparse after the first two.

Pringle worked his way across to me. 'You're not applauding enthusiastically, Governor. Are you a secret music lover?'

'Not at all. I just have no great love of lute players.'

'Ah, then we are kindred spirits. I won't have them in the regiment.'

'No?'

'There's something unmanly about it all. You can't be too careful,' Pringle added, before winking at me and walking away, a risky affair since he only had one eye which he had momentarily closed voluntarily.

I am abstemious by habit, and try to avoid overindulgence in wine or spirits because there is nothing more unbecoming in a clergyman than public drunkenness. Well, perhaps indecent exposure runs it close, but you get my point. However, it seems grossly unfair to me that often after an evening's entertainment when I have been careful not to imbibe more than is good for me, I wake up with a thumping headache as if a pair of excitable woodpeckers are having a contest inside my skull. Meanwhile, people who were barely able to stand long enough to go home eat a hearty breakfast and appear none the worse for wear.

I had seen Pringle as the entertainment ended, when he thanked our hostess profusely for her hospitality and then handed her the goblet he had just drained, apparently mistaking her for a maid. I was not expecting to see him for a few hours after daybreak and then to enjoy a silent journey with him towards Nijmegen; yet here he was at breakfast tearing lumps off a loaf and spearing herring with his dagger, all the while counselling me to drink plenty of small beer to dilute the effects of the wine.

'There's no ladies with us so we can make water wherever we please,' he remarked.

I was having a more refined breakfast of bread and cheese when I noticed two ruffians making off with my chest in broad daylight. 'Pringle! Those men! That's my chest.'

Pringle glanced briefly at the scene. 'Aye, Governor. They're my men. They've done your packing for you. No time to waste. You'll want to check your room to see they haven't overlooked anything. And if the bedclothes are missing we'd best give them back. In a place like this they're probably lousy anyway.'

I wish he had said that before I spent a night under them. For several minutes I imagined itches on all parts of my body.

Biesma settled the account and we formed up in procession for my exit from Amsterdam. This was accompanied by clods of earth from the locals until Pringle roared that the next man to throw anything would be looking at a stump where his arm used to be, at which point they switched to verbal abuse. I am pleased to say that I could not understand most of it, since their diction was not of the highest quality, but what I heard was singularly uninventive and highly disrespectful to my cloth.

I was, however, impressed by Pringle, who singlehandedly returned volley for volley, much of it in terms that I took to be some Scottish dialect or other and some of which, while colourful, was anatomically unlikely. We marched out through the city gates at which point Pringle gave his troops the order to break wind, which many of them did. I was not aware that this was a military manoeuvre but it was very effective in ensuring that we were not followed, though I believe that the soldiers at the back may have suffered terribly.

Pringle told me that by hard marching he hoped to make Amersfoort by nightfall; if the weather turned against us, we might have to settle for Soest or Baarn. William had a lodge at Soestdijk which might be convenient, having plenty of grass for horses and elegant rooms for officers. If by the word lodge you are thinking of a small wooden hut for gamekeepers, put such thoughts aside. This was a small palace and not inferior in any way to his quarters in The Hague. In fact, William preferred Soestdijk, partly because he enjoyed exercise and because his breathing was better in the country. In the event we left the men at Baarn while a few officers and I trudged the last few miles to Soestdijk after supper; only to find the gates locked and no-one there to receive us. Pringle offered to break a window so we could gain entry, but I declined and said I would sooner sleep in the carriage.

And so to bed.

CHAPTER EIGHT

I will not weary the reader with a full description of the rest of my journey to Nijmegen, which can only be as tedious to read as it was to experience at the time. We were up and on the road shortly after dawn, which I suppose means that those soldiers left at Baarn must have stirred during the hours of darkness. The weather was better, and the horses found a good road, with the result that we made Randwijk, leaving us a morning's journey into Nijmegen the next day.

As we marched along, Pringle regaled me with more of his never-ending fund of stories, some of them highly unsuitable for a clergyman's ears, and some so vividly told that I had no appetite for dinner. I am rather squeamish and could never have made a soldier. I suppose it becomes easier to stab an adversary in the guts when you know he is about to do the same to you, but I abhor bloodshed and would much rather settle disputes with a debate, ideally in Latin. [No, Van der Meer, I am not going to share any of Pringle's more colourful tales. But I will say that if Pringle is to be believed there is a place called Leith in Scotland where, it appears, young women are extremely accommodating and extraordinarily supple.]

I was sitting in the carriage facing forwards — I had found that facing the other way made me feel somewhat bilious — with the result that as we approached Nijmegen I saw the most extraordinary sight. The fields were filled with men in tents. I do not know how many live in Nijmegen, but there must have been nearly as many outside the city as in it. As we rode forward many sprang to their feet and saluted. Whether this was due to Pringle's uniform or the fact that someone in a carriage must be a man of importance, I do not know, but it made a welcome change from being pelted with Amsterdam mud.

We paused while Pringle exchanged some words with a couple of officers, then we moved forward through the city gates. Whether it is natural or man-made, I cannot say, but the principal buildings of the city stand on a hill, an unusual sight in our country, and as we approached the city they were mightily imposing. It meant, however, that our progress through the city involved a climb which slowed us down quite a bit.

We came to a halt outside the Town Hall, a magnificent façade in front of a higgledy-piggledy concatenation of rooms. It seems that the building originally consisted of some large houses which were brought together and remodelled, not altogether harmoniously.

Pringle and I entered. The aldermen had been hastily assembled as we approached and were waiting for us in a large hall where wine and a table of meats had been set up to refresh us. By the look of the table they had been expecting to have to feed our entire company of two thousand. I detected some apprehension in the air.

A large man stepped forward to introduce himself. I presume he was the mayor, since he wore a fur mantle and a large gold chain (though not as large as mine).

'Governor Mercurius, I bid you welcome. I hope your journey was not too tedious.'

I had a choice. I could tell the truth or I could keep the atmosphere pleasant. 'Thank you, not too bad,' I said.

I was introduced to the aldermen. It is as well that this was done, because if I had encountered them after dark I should have taken them for footpads or similar ruffians. We exchanged a few words and sat down to eat together.

Any native of Leiden can tell you that during the famous siege in 1574 the mayor, Van der Werff, refused to surrender to the Spanish, telling the starving inhabitants that they could eat his arm if necessary. On that basis the people of Nijmegen were in no danger of starvation, for the mayor alone could feed a family for a week, provided they were fond of lard, and he had an appetite to match. I ate sparingly as usual and spent much of the time trying to avoid disclosing my mission in the face of persistent questioning.

'Will your troops be here long, Governor?' the mayor enquired.

'They're not my troops,' I pointed out. 'They are the Stadhouder's men.'

'I recognise that there may be some secrecy necessary,' the mayor continued, 'but it would be helpful to know how long they will be here. They're eating us out of house and home.' This said while he demolished a roast chicken singlehandedly, mark you.

'How much do you know already?' I asked.

Out of the corner of my eye I saw Pringle put his goblet down and attend closely to our conversation for fear, I suppose, that I might give too much away.

'The Stadhouder told us that he was assembling his army here; that you were appointed Governor of Moers and would take them with you when you departed.'

I relaxed. I need say no more.

'That is correct. I am told that the journey to Moers will take two to three days. Since I cannot know what stores await us there it would be helpful if the men could be supplied with a week's rations.'

The mayor looked shocked. 'We might manage four days, but some have been here for nearly a week already.'

Four days would suit me quite well, but I was not going to allow this pudding to dictate to me. After all, I was a Governor and he was a mere mayor.

'Well, shall we say five days? I have no wish to impose upon you any more.'

'I assume, then, that now that you are here, their departure is imminent.'

'Not necessarily,' I replied. 'I shall move on tomorrow to make arrangements to receive the army in Moers, and my escort will travel with me. But the rest of the army is not under my command and its general will decide when it moves.'

Pringle smiled. I must have inadvertently said the right thing. I had, incidentally, no idea who was commanding the army pending the arrival of the Stadhouder, nor the least notion when William would arrive. I only hoped that I would have left before he did so, because my job was complicated enough without any additional brainwaves that might have occurred to him since we had last met.

The meal being concluded, I made to rise from the table with our host, when he spoke words that chilled me to the very marrow.

'Since you are leaving tomorrow, perhaps you would do me the honour of attending a small lute concert this evening? There's a special treat — we have engaged an Italian opera singer.'

'Oh, joy,' I said.

Pringle suddenly remembered that his horse needed shoeing that evening. As we left the room I exchanged a few words with him. I will not record them here.

I do not think that lute music is particularly mentioned in the Bible as one of the miseries inflicted upon the damned in Hell, but if it isn't it should be, especially when, as here, it is played by someone who appears to have only taken up the instrument a week or two before. We were also "entertained", and I allow that word its widest possible meaning, by a group of schoolboys who sang some local folk songs, evidence, if it were needed, that the local folk lead lives of the greatest misery and, to judge by the tune, extreme pain.

The opera singer was the same one who had tormented us in Amsterdam and I instructed Biesma to make sure that his tour did not include a diversion to Moers. Still, there were a number of tasty delicacies, which led me to wonder, very briefly, how Albrecht was recovering. I meant him no ill-will, because he was a helpful and friendly man, but I hoped that the surgeons would tell him that he had recovered well but would never cook again. I then repented of so unworthy and vindictive a thought and it is not impossible that what happened to me later in this tale was my penance for behaving so badly.

I slept very ill, possibly because my bed was too soft. I am not accustomed to luxury. It might also have been due to an excess of sugar in the sweetmeats, a guilty conscience after my thoughts about Albrecht, or my fury at Pringle slinking off in the evening, and when I was dressed and ready I made a point of examining his horse's hooves to see if he really had been reshod. The scoundrel had anticipated me, and I found myself looking at shiny new shoes on immaculately trimmed hooves.

'I wasn't aware that you were a farrier, Governor, or I could have saved some money,' Pringle said.

'I have shoed a horse in my time,' I replied. It was true. It was also around thirty-five years earlier. My grandfather taught me to do it.

I climbed into my carriage, and acknowledged the cheers of the city council of Nijmegen as I left them in peace. Believe me, however happy they were to see the back of me, I was just as grateful to shake the dust of Nijmegen from my feet.

So at last we came to Moers. A messenger from William had informed them of my appointment and since a troop of horse, a carriage and a baggage train are hard to sneak into a city, they had enough notice of our arrival to arrange a bit of a welcoming ceremony.

Moers is an unusual city in many ways. It is, so far as I can tell, surrounded by water like a large moat, and heavily fortified, with several emplacements for cannon on its walls and a large castle at its centre. Being surrounded by Germany, the locals speak mainly German, though some of the better sort are also proficient in Dutch; as for the rest, they proceed from an assumption that Dutchmen are simply Germans with the brains knocked out and therefore speak to us very slowly in pidgin German. Take a seat in a tavern and you will be asked 'You want big beer, little beer? Also something to eat?' At an early stage I put a stop to this nonsense by declaring that I would speak Latin to those who could and we got along a lot better after that.

Descending from my carriage I was a little perturbed to find Pringle standing beside the steps with a sword drawn.

'You can't be too careful, Governor,' he whispered. 'I haven't had a chance to search them. If you see anyone you want killing, just tip me the wink.'

'I'm not sure I can just go around killing the Stadhouder's subjects at my whim,' I replied.

'Oh, you can,' Pringle assured me. 'I've read the paperwork. About halfway down the second page.'

A little girl advanced towards me holding a bunch of flowers. I quickly glanced at Pringle to reassure myself that he was not going to run her through, but apart from taking a step closer he seemed content that I should receive the bouquet. She curtseyed prettily and I thanked her.

'What is your name, child?' I asked.

There came no reply and she looked helplessly at someone I took to be her mother. She, in turn, looked helplessly at a slender man in a blue gown, who bent over the girl and whispered some words of German in her ear. She brightened and curtseyed again.

'Johanna, *wenn es Ihnen gefällt, Exzellenz*.'

This phrase, which I may not have recorded correctly, was one I was to hear regularly. It means 'if it please Your Excellency' and the people of Moers tacked it on all kinds of statements, especially if they knew that it would not please my excellency; I grew tired of hearing things like 'three more peasants died of the plague, if it please Your Excellency' or 'the tower privy is blocked again, if it please Your Excellency'.

At this point a sphere with inadequate arms and legs attached stepped forward and read something to me from a scroll, of which I understood very little, but then he repeated it in Latin, from which I gathered it to be an address of welcome assuring me of the loyalty of the population to the Prince of Orange. They never called him the Stadhouder, which was reasonable enough since, so far as they were concerned, the Stadhoudership was irrelevant. He was their prince as Prince of Orange.

The globule turned out to be the mayor, who was sweating profusely under his long fur mantle.

'If it comes to it, I'll hang that one,' muttered Pringle. 'God knows what will escape if I pierce his belly.'

The man in the blue gown then stepped forward and addressed me in immaculate Latin. He introduced himself as Eberhard Fleckstein, undersecretary to the previous Governor and acting secretary. This was a complication that I had not envisaged, since I had earmarked Biesma for the role of secretary, though I was bound to recognise that someone who spoke German would be an advantage when one is administering a German population. On the spot I promoted Biesma to the newly-created role of administrator of my private office, at which he seemed satisfied, and told Fleckstein we would sort out how the two roles related to each other in due course, while hoping that I would be gone before it became an issue. After all, Biesma and I were only going to be there a couple of months.

The mayor spoke again. His name was Tobias Schmidt but since there were many Schmidts in town he was universally known as Mayor Tobias. He delivered the appalling news that in honour of my arrival they had arranged a small banquet. Since this was still being cooked, it would be preceded by a musical entertainment.

'Just issue the order,' Pringle murmured, 'and I'll cut the fingers off all the lutenists in town.'

In fact, the musical entertainment was much better than I feared, with not a stringed instrument in sight. A group of people played on flutes and recorders while someone kept time with a small drum, then a girl played very prettily on a shawm, after which she was joined by men playing sackbuts and fagotts. I had never seen a fagott before. It is rather like a shawm but of extreme length to give a low note, and is therefore bent back on itself as otherwise the player would need to be about eight feet tall. It is, of course, possible that my appreciation of the entertainment was enhanced by the excellent white wine provided, a servant being detailed to stand behind me and refill my beaker whenever there was room to top it up. If I had not been alert I might have passed my entire time in Moers in a drunken stupor.

As the banquet was about to start Pringle approached me. 'I must see to my men, Governor. Take this.' He handed me an item in a leather pouch.

'What is it?'

'A fish-gutting knife. Much more sure than a short-bladed dagger. I'll be back as soon as possible but I don't want to leave you unprotected. You may eat freely — I've tried all the food. But just in case they've pulled a trick on me, wait until someone else has sampled a dish before you swallow.'

I am a university lecturer. I haunt libraries. The risk of imminent assassination is not something I had previously needed to guard against, even in the most heated philosophical debates. I am also a priest, and the Church is rather opposed to us going around armed. My knowledge of such things was more or less limited to being aware that one holds the handle and shoves the pointy end into one's opponent. I could only hope he wouldn't bleed much, or I might swoon and be murdered while unconscious; though, on reflection, perhaps that is the best way to be murdered.

At the banquet both the local Reformed minister and the Catholic priest said a grace before we sat down. This was rather competitive, each attempting to outdo the other, so we were on our feet for a while, but eventually they finished and the youth at my shoulder immediately poured me a beaker of wine.

Whatever appetite I might have had had been much diminished by Pringle's mention of poison, and I caused some consternation by asking for a piece of bread from the loaf along the table rather than the untouched one in front of me, but one can never be too careful. I explained my actions by saying that it was my habit not to begin any food that had not already been sampled so as to reduce the risk of waste, which was a great sin. All nodded sympathetically and Mayor Tobias looked sheepish. I thought for a moment that he was going to try to reattach the chicken leg he had just torn off.

I realised that I was expected to say a few words, so I asked Fleckstein if he would translate my Latin, and took a large draught of wine to steady my nerves. Unhappily, some of it went down the wrong way and I had a coughing fit as a result. This was the point at which Pringle, who had slipped in unnoticed, charged forward with his sword drawn and demanded to know who had given me the wine. It was all I could do to assure him that it was not poisoned, but just to be on the safe side he drained my beaker — which the lad at once refilled.

I thanked them for their welcome, assured them of my goodwill and that of the Prince of Orange, and apologised in advance for the necessary privations that I was compelled by my orders to place upon them. Since I did not know how loyal they were I dared not tell them that the army would shortly be marching through on its way to mount a surprise attack on France, but neither could I give any explanation for demanding food for twenty thousand men except to say that it was the express command of William that I issue decrees to gather in food for the army's use. It might have been, I suppose, that the food was then to be shipped to Nijmegen since it was common knowledge that the army was mustering there, it being rather hard to hide twenty thousand men, and it was also known that I had just come from there.

I concluded by saying that I had much to do and proposed to get to work at once, and then raised my beaker to propose the health and prosperity of all present.

'Unless they're traitors, of course,' added Pringle *sotto voce*.

CHAPTER NINE

The alert reader will notice that up to this point there has been no crime. That is true in one sense, but not in another, because the crime had occurred around the time I left Leiden, but I did not yet know of it.

We took up our quarters in the castle. My private suite was well-appointed with a bedchamber, in which there was a magnificent bed with a crimson velvet canopy and curtains. It was large enough to absorb a family, and though I was unmarried there was a second room for my children. One of the beds in there seemed rather more comfortable so I decided to use that one.

Pringle was a few doors down the corridor, and Biesma next door to him. Fleckstein and his family lived in one of the attics; occasionally I heard his small daughters running around above me. I love the sound of happy children playing. It is bittersweet because I will never have children of my own, but it softens the heart and distracts the troubled mind to hear them.

I washed myself and walked to the large chamber that was to be my workplace. There was a small table at which Biesma was sitting, though I believe that Fleckstein had been using it and cast envious eyes upon it. My first thought was to banish Fleckstein to the anteroom, but then it occurred to me that he would be able to control who had access to me and who did not, so my second thought was that Biesma should really be there, with Fleckstein in the room so I could keep an eye upon him. Then I had a third thought, which was really more or less the first thought dressed up slightly differently, and then I decided that this decision-making lark was a lot harder than I had previously supposed.

It was in this paralysed state that Pringle found me. He walked in without knocking, but since the door was open I suppose it was of no consequence.

'You look pensive, Governor.'

'I am. Let us withdraw to some quiet corner where we can have a private discussion.'

He followed me to the window where I explained my quandary.

'There is a desk there which Biesma is sitting at but Fleckstein has been using and covets.'

'Isn't coveting someone's desk against one of the Ten Commandments?'

'Well, coveting generally,' I conceded. 'Desks aren't specifically mentioned.'

'So what's the problem?'

'If I give it to Biesma, Fleckstein will be outside and will control access to me. If I give it to Fleckstein, Biesma will feel slighted and I'll have someone in the room I don't really know. I can't decide.'

'I can,' Pringle announced. 'Chuck them both out and have the whole room to yourself.'

'But the desk is here.'

'Desks can be moved. Besides, to send them out is in accordance with one of the key principles of successful governorship.'

He intrigued me. For a moment I almost thought he knew what he was talking about.

Pringle put a hand on my shoulder in a fatherly way, though I suspect he must have been about my age. 'Allow me to explain, Governor.'

'I wish you would.'

'Let us suppose that you are a prince or king somewhere. It doesn't matter where. What is your greatest fear?'

'Louis XIV?' I proposed tentatively. I had been spending too long with the Stadhouder.

'No, besides him.'

I shrugged my shoulders. I am very wary of bats, but I doubted that this was the answer he was hoping for.

'Why, assassination! As king, you are a constant target for those who would be king. Now, let us further suppose that you have two treacherous sons, each of whom would like to be king. Which do you name as your successor?'

'The one I like better?'

Pringle laughed. 'Very droll. No, you don't name either. As soon as you name one, the other becomes your enemy; and his brother will oppose him, of course, but will bear no particular love for you because it is in his own interest that something terrible should befall you. In one stroke you have converted two potential enemies into actual enemies and done yourself no good. This is where you must be cunning, Governor. Never name a number two, because number twos soon get to thinking that they should be number ones. Name two number twos, and then they will devote their energies to keeping an eye on each other, thus ensuring your safety.'

I applied this lesson to my current circumstances. 'So if I send them both into the anteroom, they will each check that the other is not abusing his position and I will get some peace?'

'Bravo! I knew you were a quick learner. One of the benefits of being a university man.'

He said this in a tone that conveyed to me his suspicion that there were no other conceivable benefits to a university man; and I might, in other circumstances, have bridled at the suggestion that I was a quick learner because I had gone to the university, as opposed to having gone to the university because I was a quick learner. However, I was so delighted to have made a decision that I ignored this fallacy and immediately gave the requisite orders, while adding that my door would normally stand open and that they had equal rights of access to me.

With them gone Pringle produced a sheet of paper from his sleeve.

'What is this?' I asked.

'It is the list of supplies that the army will need. You'll need to have one of your secretaries draw up the necessary decrees.'

I glanced over it. 'How much?' I gasped.

'You can't expect soldiers to fight and die on an empty stomach,' Pringle explained.

'They won't be doing much fighting,' I said. 'They'll be too busy gorging themselves at the table.'

Pringle tried to curb his impatience. 'Twenty thousand men need a lot of food, Governor. Each will need a loaf of bread every day, and half a gallon of beer. Then the horses need feeding…'

In no time he had given me the feeling that I was being parsimonious by only allowing them three meals a day.

'…and each man with a gun will need a pound of powder and some lead bullets.'

'Where am I going to get those?' I wailed.

'That is not your concern, Governor. You need only give the order, and then leave your underlings to worry about where they are to be found. If I may make a suggestion, it is my experience that these requisitions proceed much more smoothly if you undertake to hang anyone who attempts to impede them.'

'It would be monstrous to hang a man because he wanted to keep a basket of turnips to feed his family, Captain.'

'Your compassion does you credit, Governor. And I suppose if there are no turnips the horses will starve and the soldiers could eat them. But how would the Stadhouder view the matter?'

This was his trump card. If I knew the Stadhouder, William would gladly go without food for a few days if it meant an extra barrel of powder for his troops, and he expected everyone else to feel the same way. Reluctantly, I called Biesma in and instructed him to draw up the necessary decrees.

'When do you want them, Governor?' he asked.

'I'll take and proclaim each one as you finish it. Don't bother waiting for the ink to dry,' Pringle said. 'We need to get on with this if we are to be ready when the army comes.'

When he left I was profoundly depressed. I felt that I was being forced to commit acts that I would not ordinarily have countenanced, and that would make me hated amongst the populace. But I had no choice if I were to fulfil my orders.

A gentle cough disturbed my self-pity. Looking up, I saw Fleckstein standing over me with some papers in his hand.

'Yes?' I asked.

'Some papers requiring your signature, Governor. Small administrative matters left in abeyance when the last Governor departed.'

He handed me the papers and dipped my pen in the inkhorn before handing it to me and indicating the place at which I should sign.

'A moment, Fleckstein. I'm not signing something I haven't read.'

'As you wish, Governor,' he said, while arching an eyebrow gently as if to suggest that this policy was a considerable divergence from that of my predecessor.

'Fleckstein, this is an execution warrant.'

'Indeed, Governor.'

'And so is this. And this. And this.'

'Ah, forgive me, Governor, but the fourth one is merely an order to chop a hand off. Not an actual execution, as such.'

'Have these people had trials?'

Fleckstein sucked the air through his teeth very hard as if I had suggested something improper. 'Trials, Governor?'

'Yes, trials. You know, before a judge.'

'You are the chief magistrate here now, Governor. That is why I have brought them to you for signature.'

'So they haven't been before a judge?'

'Unlike the Prince's other territories, judges do not visit us here. You fulfil that role.'

'And did my predecessor conduct a hearing?'

'No, Governor. If he had, he would have signed their death warrants immediately.'

'Have they confessed?'

'Yes, no, no and yes.'

'Yet despite the confession you have not proceeded to punishment as the law permits.'

'It requires the consent of the mayor or leading civic dignitary, Governor.'

'Indeed it does. And who is he?'

'You, Governor. As Governor you also chair the council. Nobody would dare sign this and usurp your authority.'

I laid the pen down. 'Presumably they have been in jail some time, Fleckstein. What is the hurry?'

'No hurry, Governor. It's just that it'll soon be time for the fair and the locals like to end the day with a good hanging. It draws the crowds to town.'

'This is appalling, Fleckstein! Condemned criminals are not to be used for sport. I will not sign these until I am acquainted with all the circumstances of their cases. Bring me the papers and I will consider them carefully.'

He bowed politely, though I could hear his teeth grinding. I would read each one carefully and see if I could not find a reason to acquit them. In my time my enquiries had brought people to the gallows and I hated that knowledge. I would gladly have avoided it if it had been in my power, so the reader can well imagine how I felt about signing an actual death warrant.

I took a sheet of paper from a drawer and began drafting a letter of resignation. It would save time later if I prepared it now.

Fleckstein brought me the four reports. They were scandalously brief, but even in their abbreviated form they made uncomfortable reading.

Calvin Wisse was the first case I took up. He had confessed to killing a man called Donk in a tavern brawl and had been proposed for hanging. I say proposed rather than sentenced because this appeared to be an administrative rather than a judicial decision. Someone sitting at a table had simply applied the rule that those who kill, hang, and set the wheels in motion.

'I should like to see this man Wisse,' I said to Fleckstein.

'Is that sensible? He's a criminal. I cannot vouch for your safety.'

'I will take the chance. If need be I'll go to his cell.'

'He doesn't have a cell. Well, not a personal one. We only have two proper cells in the prison so the men are in one and the women in the other.'

'Then perhaps he can be brought to me.'

'He's none too sanitary, Governor.'

'Hardly his fault, if you're going to hold all the men in one cell, is it? I'll see him in the garden, then.'

'He might escape, Governor. The garden has quite low walls.'

'Is he shackled?'

'Of course. You can't allow murderers to walk around freely.'

'Then I don't think a man in shackles is going to find it easy to scale a wall, Fleckstein.'

If you can bow doubtfully, that is what Fleckstein did. A sort of hesitant 'Well don't say I didn't warn you' bow.

Wisse was presently brought before me in the garden. To say he was insanitary was an understatement. I could smell him from five paces. I had brought Biesma with me to make some notes and I saw him recoil.

'Fleckstein, could we please have some water and a towel so mijnheer Wisse can wash himself?'

Wisse looked astonished but stammered his thanks. Fleckstein clearly thought that this was an excess of charity, but bowed cursorily and stalked off to find an underling to order around.

'How are you being treated?' I asked Wisse.

'I'm ill fed, and I've got lice,' he replied, 'but I am not maltreated.'

'Lice? Where do the lice come from?'

'I don't know, Governor. I suppose it has something to do with all the rats.'

I was appalled. Being sentenced to hang is one thing, but inflicting lice on prisoners was no part of the sentence. I acknowledge that lice get everywhere, and there were one or two of the undergraduates at Leiden I would keep at a distance, but by and large we Dutch are a clean people, particularly the women. Dutch women are rarely seen without a broom close at hand and as you walk down a street you will see doors open as dust is expelled and bedclothes are aired. I recall a dispute in Steen's Inn when one of the customers called Fat Lysbeth a 'snaggle-toothed pox-ridden dirty old whore' and she screamed 'Who are you calling dirty?' and broke a bottle of genever over his head, such was her objection to being labelled with that word.

I digress. I asked Biesma to make a note to ask Pringle for some soldiers to guard the prisoners in the garden while the cells were given a thorough cleaning. I also asked for a mason to plug any holes by which rats might enter. After all, the dungeons were under my quarters and I did not like the thought of such vermin in what was now my home, albeit for as short a time as I could wangle.

Wisse, now rather more presentable, knelt before me.

'Tell me what happened when Donk was killed. Did you know him before?'

Wisse nodded, apparently too emotional to speak at first. 'He was one of my best friends.'

'A friend? And yet you killed him?'

'I did, Governor. I did not mean to do so, but I did it, may God have mercy on my soul.'

'What caused the brawl?'

Wisse looked confused. 'Brawl, Governor? What brawl?'

'The tavern brawl in which Donk met his end.'

'There was no brawl. It happened in a tavern, certainly, but there was no brawl.'

'Then describe the incident to me.'

'We had been drinking, that is true, and perhaps we had taken more than was good for us, though I would not say that I was drunk.'

'And Donk?'

'He had taken more than me and had become boisterous.'

'And what form did that take?'

'He mounted a bench and proclaimed that he could hold the bench against anyone for nobody could push him off it.'

'And did many try?'

'Oh, yes, Governor. At least three before me. They climbed on the bench and Donk would push them off. He was a big man, Governor, a forester used to swinging a heavy axe.'

'And what happened when you tried?'

'Well, I reasoned that nobody could push him off, because he was heavier than any of us and had a long reach, so when he stretched out an arm towards me I grabbed it and pulled. As I expected, he lost his balance and I buffeted his shoulder with mine, and he fell off.'

'What happened next?'

'He lay face down on the floor and did not move. He moaned a little but never spoke again. I think he must have struck his head on the stone flags of the tavern floor.'

'Thank you. Have you anything to say in your defence?'

'Only that I meant Donk no harm and I am heartily sorry for it. I know by the law I must die and I am ready to pay the penalty for my crime, if you will graciously allow me a priest to minister to me.'

'Master Fleckstein, why was this man condemned? What law does he refer to?'

'Why, Governor, the common law of the land. God's law. An eye for an eye and a tooth for a tooth.'

'I see. And do you still stone adulteresses to death?'

'No, Governor, that would be barbaric. We simply return them to their husband for him to deal with as he wishes. They are, after all, his property. It would be unthinkable to deprive a man of his private possessions. If he chooses to destroy them himself, of course, that is quite different.'

I know I keep digressing, but I will do so again. Just a short time before this incident I had been sent to Maastricht to take part in a debate. There I had met the Abbess Mathilde, a nun of some reputation and striking appearance, who, through any tribulation or circumstance, maintained an impenetrable air of calm faith. I had resolved to try to emulate this example by avoiding any strong passions, but at this moment I was failing completely in this aim. If any man had ventured to tell my grandmother that she was my grandfather's chattel I would not give a bent pin for his safety, and serve him right too. One of the objectives of marriage is to enjoy each other's company, and even the Apostle Paul, who could be quite old-fashioned about women sometimes, allowed that marriage is a good thing for both sexes. It is hard to see that a lifetime of near-slavery could be good for the woman.

'Fleckstein, explain to me why this man deserves to hang.'

'He committed a voluntary act that led to a death.'

'Indeed, but he did not intend to kill.'

'But he intended the act that caused the death, therefore he is guilty of it.'

I have no legal training, and some lawyers reading this may be nodding and telling me I know nothing. Well, I have no medical training either, but I know when my leg is broken. As a philosopher and debater, I knew what to say next. 'So if a farmer kills a pig for meat, do we hang him?'

'By no means.'

'But he is intending an act that leads to death.'

'Not a human death.'

'Let us then be precise. It is not life that matters, but human life.'

'Correct.'

'So, Master Fleckstein, if I see a man about to stab the Prince of Orange and I run him through with my sword, will you hang me?'

This was an entirely hypothetical argument. I don't know what I would do if I saw someone about to stab the Prince, but physical violence is well down my list of options. I would probably shout a warning to the Prince and employ vicious sarcasm on the would-be assassin. One must play to one's strengths.

'No, Governor. You are serving a higher purpose.'

'Reverse it then. I see the Prince about to stab a man so I stab him first. Would you hang me then?'

'Definitely. You have stabbed the Prince.'

'Who was stabbing an innocent man.'

'No doubt the Prince would have his reasons,' Fleckstein sniffed.

'And his reasons are, *ipso facto*, better than my reasons?'

'Of course. He is the Prince.'

'That is illogical.'

'Perhaps. But it is the law.'

'If the law thinks that, the law is an ass.'

'Maybe. But it is all we have to ride.'

'And if we hang this man, Wisse, who benefits?'

'We all do. A dangerous criminal will have been removed from our midst.'

'In what sense, dangerous?'

'He is a self-confessed murderer.'

'He confessed to killing, not to murdering.'

Fleckstein made no reply.

'Mijnheer Wisse, have you any family?' I asked.

'A mother, sir, and a brother and sister.'

'How old is your brother?'

'Sixteen, sir.'

'Without your work, life must be a struggle for them.'

'It is, sir. I am heartily sorry that they are punished thus for my misdeeds.'

'So am I. And Donk? What family had he?'

'His father is living still, and his mother. He has a married sister, I believe.'

'Thank you. Fleckstein, I should like to meet Donk's parents. Could you arrange it, please?'

Fleckstein's mouth flapped like a fish out of water, but he bowed, somewhat belatedly.

I called Biesma to me and spoke softly into his ear. 'Biesma, make sure he does.'

CHAPTER TEN

The second case was even less satisfactory. A young man called Hubert Erler was brought before me and thrust to his knees. He was no more sanitary than Wisse, so I ordered him given water too.

'I have read a report of your case,' I said. 'You remained silent when questioned. You neither confess nor deny your guilt. Why?'

He shook his head and made no answer.

The facts of the matter can be briefly stated. Erler was observed by a neighbour digging a large hole in his family's farmyard. Upon investigation, his parents were found in the kitchen. They had been stabbed several times each, and with much force. Clearly the murderer was extremely angry.

Erler claimed that he had just returned home, having been inspecting a ram which he hoped to put to his ewes, but his shirt was slightly bloodstained and the fact that his parents had not cried for help was suggestive of the killer being known to them, so that they had not been on their guard. Erler was therefore arrested and brought to the castle, since which time he had said nothing.

'Who is looking after the farm?' I asked.

'The prisoner has a sister, Anna,' Fleckstein replied.

'Is she married?'

'No, but it would be most improper to take advantage of her at such a time, Governor.'

'I was not planning to debauch her, Fleckstein. Why should you reprove me so for thoughts that I have not had?'

Fleckstein mumbled an apology.

'I merely wanted to know if she has another household to keep.'

'No, Governor. She lives with the prisoner and their parents.'

'But she was not there when this took place?'

'She had gone to visit a friend, but when she arrived her friend was not at home, so she came back.'

The prisoner looked fixedly at the ground.

'Mijnheer Erler,' I said, 'please look at me.'

He did so without any hesitation.

'You must understand your position,' I continued. 'If you confess, you will be sentenced, and the usual sentence is that you be hanged by the neck until dead. If you plead not guilty you will be tried. But if you continue to make no plea then you will be tortured until you do so.'

He said nothing, but his Adam's apple betrayed a sudden gulp at the prospect of torture. I could not blame him for that. Mine was doing the same, and I was not going to be the one stretched on the rack. I had never seen a man on the rack before and had no desire to do so now, having heard the screams from the prison when I was walking to the Binnenhof in The Hague. Despite the thick prison walls, such noises can carry a long way.

'Mijnheer Erler,' I continued, 'for pity's sake plead not guilty.'

He returned to staring at the ground and refused to speak.

'He is contumacious,' Fleckstein commented. 'Shall I have the executioner show him the instruments?'

Like many places, Moers exercised economy by having the same man double as executioner and public torturer. Good executioners can make a tidy living and are much in demand. It is not unknown for a town to seduce a successful torturer from his current place with a higher salary and the promise of a house rent-free. One of the attributes of a good executioner is that they avoid the nasty part of their work by a flamboyant display of the gruesome tools of their trade. Many a prisoner is moved to confession by an exhibition of the instruments that will shortly be ripping pieces off him. If that does not work, I understand that strapping him to a chair and removing his drawers often does the trick. For some reason men are more concerned about having hot irons or rasps used on their privities than on, say, their arms. Anyway, it seemed no bad thing to let Erler know what he was in for if he remained silent, but I wanted to do whatever I could to avoid such agonies being inflicted upon him, so I beckoned Fleckstein to me with the aim of speaking softly to him so that Erler could not hear me.

'Show him the instruments, but let them not be used until I have given a definite instruction in the matter.'

Fleckstein nodded and turned away, showing altogether too much relish for what was to come than I was comfortable with; but I had to acknowledge that if Erler had indeed killed his parents there was a penalty prescribed in law and it would be my melancholy duty to pronounce it and see that it was carried out.

I watched Erler turn away and shuffle back to his cell. I hoped it would at least be cleaner than it had been, but I could not convince myself that it would ever be a pleasant place. I had some experience of imprisonment and it is my view that if every magistrate were compelled to pass one night in a dungeon they would be considerably less keen to send men there in future.

There were still two cases to review, but my spirits were depressed, so I announced a half-hour adjournment and went to my room to pray. It was a bit much to hope that I would prove that nobody had killed Erler's parents, or that each had killed the other. Someone had undoubtedly done it, and I would, in due course, have to condemn them to death for doing so; but, like Our Lord in the Garden of Gethsemane, I prayed that this cup might pass from me.

And ideally not to Fleckstein.

The third warrant proved not to be an execution warrant as such, though it might as well have been. It concerned one Alida Krul, a woman in her thirties, who had run away from her husband and made scandalous accusations concerning his treatment of her to a number of people in the nearby city of Duisburg.

'How far is it to Duisburg?' I asked Fleckstein.

'You might walk it in a morning,' he replied.

'And she was captured there?'

'Her husband followed her and took her to the mayor. But because Duisburg lies outside the county of Moers, in the Duchy of Cleves, he might not bring her home without the mayor's leave. The mayor ruled that she could be brought back but, not being conversant with the law of Moers, instructed that she must be brought to the Governor to know his pleasure in the matter.'

The Governor of Moers did not take any pleasure in the matter, but this was not the time or place to say so. 'And what does the husband seek?'

'Why, that she be returned to him for suitable chastisement.'

'Is she here now?'

'In the prison, Governor. Shall I have her brought to you?'

'If you please.'

I was deeply uneasy about this. A married woman depends upon her husband for all the necessities of life, because all her property becomes his on marriage. A few women of the better sort are able to retain rights over particular items, such as family jewellery, but that hardly applied to Alida Krul whose husband was a draper, according to the papers. It followed that if she had run away from him, she must have some great cause to do so, and until I knew what it was I was reluctant to return her to him. The difficulty was that I needed a pretext not to do so.

'The law is clear,' Biesma told me. 'She is his property and must be returned to him.'

'We will see, Biesma,' I said. 'He may intend her some harm.'

'Even so, Governor, he is entitled to harm her, just as a man might break his own looking-glass if it please him.'

'And if he kills her?'

'He loses a wife. I understand your concern, Governor, but there is nothing we can do about it. It is the law.'

The papers were not promising. At one point in his affidavit Heribert Krul noted that all her property was his, so by running away in her clothes she had committed theft, for which he wanted her branded in the main square. I began to wonder what kind of harridan was about to be presented to me.

Fleckstein reappeared, followed by a tiny woman being dragged by two guards. They flung her on the grass in front of me. They had not done this to either Wisse or Erler, and I suspected that she was used in this way solely because she was a woman, as if every man had an interest in keeping her in her place as an example to their own wives. Well, having no wife, I was not about to play that game.

'Please bring her a stool,' I ordered. 'And water to wash, and something to drink.'

Fleckstein looked at me as men must have looked at St Francis of Assisi when he spoke to the animals and birds, but complied with my request.

'Mevrouw,' I said, 'your husband is not here. You may speak freely.'

She did not reply, but looked puzzled.

'She has no Dutch, Governor,' Fleckstein explained.

'Then please tell her what I just said.'

To my untutored ear the local German dialect did not sound very different to my Dutch, but I had to concede that I understood very little of her reply.

'She thanks you for your kindness, Governor,' Fleckstein translated. [No, Van der Meer, we can dispense with all the translations from here. The intelligent reader will understand that whenever she speaks, she actually spoke German and Fleckstein translated it for me. Van der Meer merely wishes to show off that he speaks German; although, since I do not, we only have his word for that. He may be speaking drivel for all I know. After all, he usually does.]

With her face and hands washed, Alida Krul sat on the stool. She ran her fingers through her blonde hair as if to comb it, though her hair was so matted it made little difference. However, she then took the pitcher of water and poured it over her head before shaking the water out like a dog.

Before me was a woman who looked more like a child of fourteen or fifteen. Her face was older, of course, but she was slightly built with large blue eyes, sharp cheekbones and good teeth, except that she was missing one in her lower jaw. Now that I was looking more closely, I could see several scars on her forearms and the little finger of her right hand was crooked, as if it had been broken and poorly set.

'You ran away from home, mevrouw,' I said, in as kindly a tone as I could to encourage her to reply. 'Would you tell me why?'

'It is no home for me,' she snarled. 'A home should be a place of safety and comfort. I have done my best to make it so, but all I get from him is pain.'

'You speak of your husband?'

She lifted her hand. 'He broke this finger, and the one beside it. For three days I could not use this arm. He has punched me and knocked out a tooth. He has given me a black eye so that I was ashamed to go outdoors. What more need you know?'

I was at a loss for words, but before I could say anything she leapt to her feet and unbuttoned her bodice before lifting her blouse. 'See my ribs! A few days ago they were still black and blue from his beating.'

She appeared unconcerned that her right breast was exposed, but I think that her passion accounted for her immodesty. For the first time she was heard, and she was going to take full advantage of that.

While she dressed herself again I averted my eyes and quickly read Heribert Krul's accusation afresh. 'Your husband claims that your clothes are his so that you have, effectively, stolen them when you ran away.'

She laughed bitterly. 'Is that so? Well, I'd have happily run away naked if I'd known! I wonder that he is not ashamed to make such a claim and have the whole world know how he has used me. For, if I come to court, I'll tell all. I'll let the world know what he has me do in the bedchamber. And that alone will shame him in men's eyes.'

'Mevrouw, that will only lower their opinion of you too.'

'I am past caring! Let everyone in Moers know what their draper does. I'll wager no woman of any dignity will go there again.'

'You do not need to shout, mevrouw. I'm only paces from you.'

Her anger subsided. 'My apologies, Governor.'

It was at this point that she produced the most convincing point in her argument. She burst into tears.

I am utterly helpless in the face of female tears; possibly male ones as well, but I rarely encounter those, except my own. Clearly it would be improper to descend from my chair and wrap my arms around her, but I had to stop these proceedings before both of us were sobbing.

'Mevrouw, your husband cannot reach you here. I will give orders that he is not to be admitted to you. Fleckstein, have a surgeon or matron attend to this woman's injuries and pay their account from the public purse.'

'You are very kind, Governor,' she said, and forced a faint smile.

'One last question for now, mevrouw. Why did you marry him?'

She shrugged. 'My father wished it. And my mother said that Heribert might be older, but he was well-to-do, and I should not want for anything. But I do, Governor. I want for love, and affection, and kindness.'

My heart was not exactly broken, but I could feel small cracks appearing in it. I called for another adjournment so I could compose myself and check that there was plenty of beer in the kitchen ready for when this horrible day ended.

The fourth case was commendably straightforward. One Franz Kirschbaum had written a scurrilous lampoon of a pamphlet in which he defamed the Stadhouder, denied that Moers was rightfully his and called for the county to be transferred to the Electorate of Brandenburg. He had been arrested, his pamphlets burned, and he had been sentenced to have his offending right hand cut off in the main square.

'Sentenced by whom?' I asked.

'Perhaps "sentenced" is not quite the right word,' Fleckstein oozed.

'Then what, pray, is the right word?'

'I should say rather that the punishment was proposed by the constable of the prison.'

'So it is an administrative decision?'

'Say, rather, a suggestion. It has been the custom for the constable to provide guidance for the Governor on matters of crime and punishment.'

'Is this a time-honoured custom?' I demanded to know.

'Fairly recent.'

'How recent?'

'Your predecessor's time, I think.'

'Ah, so this is a custom that hasn't yet had time to become customary. And if I have anything to do with it, it never will. Mutilation as a punishment has no place in a civilised society.'

'They still cut ears off in England, Governor.'

'My point precisely. No place in a civilised society.'

Fleckstein gave one of those little coughs that officials have perfected to indicate that they have not quite finished what they have to say.

'Yes, Fleckstein?'

'With all due respect, Governor —' a phrase usually employed immediately before a wanton display of disrespect — 'surely such unpatriotic sentiments cannot go unpunished, or men will feel that they can write anything they like.'

'And what would be wrong with that?'

'Well, just think. People might be confused by inadequate arguments and seduced into treason.'

'People might be grown-up enough to make their own minds up as to whether the arguments are inadequate or not.'

As I was saying this I realised the catastrophic weakness in my argument. Anyone who has seen the most recent intake of undergraduates at Leiden might doubt whether they were able to distinguish sound good sense from fantastic schemes. Unfortunately, intelligence is not a requirement for matriculation at Leiden, despite my arguments over the years. Call me old-fashioned, but if a man cannot perform simple arithmetic and construct a basic declarative sentence in Latin then I am not sure that he ought to be at a university, however rich his father may be. [Van der Meer has just asked me how I account for my fellow lecturer Master Hubertus. I grant that Hubertus is wild-eyed, that his beard and hair appear not to have seen a comb these ten years and that he dresses as if he has been attacked by footpads, but he is an utterly brilliant mathematician. And he was wild-eyed and unkempt as a young man.]

Fleckstein was not giving up. 'The Prince of Orange has been traduced. He would not wish such an act to go unpunished.'

'It is too trivial a matter for a man to lose his hand. Have you met the Prince of Orange, Fleckstein?'

'I have not had that honour, Governor.'

'I thought not. I have, on several occasions, including very recently when he sent me here. And I have no doubt at all that if he met this fellow Kirschbaum he would just tear up his pamphlet, cuff him about the ear, and think no more about it.'

Fleckstein's face showed that he was not convinced. I did not like the man, but I needed him. I did not wish to antagonise him this early in my governorship, so instead I sought to compromise with him.

'You have convinced me that some punishment is warranted, but not this one. I shall give the matter some thought.'

He bowed, recognising, I think, my implacability in the matter, not to mention the fact that dinner was ready and we were all rather hungry, so I adjourned once more and we all retired indoors.

CHAPTER ELEVEN

I will not resort to the wine flask every time I have a bad day, I told myself. After all, the way things looked at that moment I would be having a goodly number of bad days while acting as Governor, and I was not sure that any land benefits from being ruled by one who is persistently sozzled, though I am aware that several countries have involuntarily made the experiment.

My mood was not improved by Pringle's industry. Armed with assorted documents that he and Biesma had drafted for me, he had ransacked the town and was working his way round the country gathering stores for the army. As fast as grain was harvested he requisitioned it, even claiming corn still growing in the fields. As a result I was receiving petitions and complaints from a number of landowners and tenant farmers, most of them appallingly written.

'Look at all these!' I exclaimed to Biesma. 'Is there no way of softening the blow?'

Biesma took the documents and glanced over them. 'If I may say so, Governor, you would save yourself some effort if you did not bother to correct their spelling and grammar.'

'I'm a university lecturer, Biesma. It's what I do.'

'The problem is a simple one, Governor. The Stadhouder wants food for twenty thousand men for a few days. That is not a small request. Toes must be stepped on.'

'What about these people complaining that their blankets have been taken?'

'Soldiers need something to keep them warm, Governor. They are sleeping in the fields for the most part and a blanket is then a necessity.'

'And when the war is over, will they be returned?'

'That would be impractical, Governor.'

'Why?'

'It would require lists to be kept of whose blanket was given to whom; we frequently wrap corpses in blankets if we run out of shrouds; and frankly you wouldn't want a blanket back if a soldier has been using it for any length of time. It will probably be flea-ridden.'

I might have argued on this matter, since the blankets in some of the inns I have slept in were flea-ridden even in the absence of soldiers, but I could see his point. I confess that my main concern was that I was becoming very unpopular, and I could understand why, though I was, in my eyes, innocent of any malign design. I was only obeying orders.

I took up the papers relating to the four cases that I had heard. None of them was satisfactory. Was it just to hang Wisse for the accidental killing of Donk? No witness claimed that there had been any malice such that Donk's death was intentional. Accidents happen, and a terrible outcome does not prove that someone was reckless or negligent.

My mind clawed back through memories to an incident many years before. One of Leiden's leading citizens had bought a pony for his young daughter to ride, and for no known reason the pony had shied suddenly and thrown the girl off, causing horrible injuries from which she died. No-one suggested hanging the pony, yet it seemed to me to be a very similar matter to Wisse's case. How were Donk's family helped if Wisse hanged? To my unlawyerly mind it just seemed to be piling waste upon waste.

Then there was that fellow Kirschbaum. Whatever he had written, were words ever sufficiently damaging to justify maiming someone so that they would never write again? Men lose hands in battle, or in accidents at work, but to remove one coldly and deliberately seemed unjustifiable to me. Moreover, knowing William as I did, I could not imagine that he cared one whit what anyone thought of him. Actual plotting was a different matter, of course, so I would have to read Kirschbaum's pamphlet to see what he had said.

It was at this point that I hit a snag. Fleckstein had done such a good job of gathering up and burning the pamphlets that there were none left for me to read. On the one hand, this was a good thing; whatever offence they might have contained was surely extinguished in the flames. On the other hand, it was harder to exonerate someone when the evidence had been destroyed.

Alida Krul troubled me. Whatever the law might say, how could I order her returned to a husband who had hurt her before, would doubtless do so again and might one day kill her, particularly if it had been demonstrated that the law was on his side? I had no doubt that wives could be annoying on occasion. I remembered my grandfather raging at my grandmother during an argument that he wished he had never married her, to which she replied that if he had not, he would have been a sad old bachelor because there were no other idiots like her around. They were capable of great affection for each other despite my grandfather's fecklessness, but a loveless marriage must be a terrible thing. For one thing, holy scripture commands it to be otherwise, for in the Epistle to the Ephesians, the fifth chapter, we read "Husbands, love your wives", and a like instruction appears in the Epistle to the Colossians, the third chapter. That it appears twice shows us how important this teaching is, and there are other similar imperative verses if I could only remember them. I was determined not to return her to danger, but I could not think of any guarantee that might satisfy me that the peril was past.

But the case that troubled me most was that of Hubert Erler. He was an enigma. He refused to confess his sin and thereby save his soul, if not his body, but at the same time he offered no explanation that would exonerate him. What on earth was going through his young head?

On top of that, the evidence as presented was remarkably thin. He had been caught red-handed burying the bodies of his parents; but nobody had suggested any reason for strife between them. To be fair, there seemed to be little evidence because nobody had thought it was necessary to collect any. Well, if there had been no investigation at the time, I had to conduct one now, difficult as that would be. I would make no decision in his case until I had collected and weighed the facts for myself.

Fleckstein hated unfinished business, to which end he asked me yet again whether I had signed the warrants.

'Stop asking, Fleckstein! I will sign them if, and only if, I am satisfied that it is the right thing for me to do.'

I do not know if it is possible to bow in a surly and disrespectful way, but I think Fleckstein did so then.

'Are you sure that there is not a single copy of Kirschbaum's pamphlet anywhere for me to read?'

'None, Governor,' he said proudly.

'Then how am I to judge whether or not the words in them were libellous or seditious?'

'Through the testimony of those who have read them, Governor.'

'And have you read them?'

'Certainly. How else could I judge them to be libellous?'

I thought for a moment or two then rummaged around on my desk for a particular piece of paper. 'Read this,' I commanded.

Fleckstein arched his eyebrows a little in surprise but did as he was bidden.

'You have read it?' I said as he handed it back to me.

'Yes, Governor.'

'What does it say?'

'That you are to gather and store provisions for an army of twenty thousand men who will pass through here on the way to their destination, to report on any enemy movements that come to your notice, to recruit such prudent persons as may seem to you to be fitting and necessary to achieve these tasks and to remunerate them at your pleasure within an overall sum, to minister justice and carry out all the other duties of a Governor.'

'What about horses?'

'Governor?'

'You didn't mention horses. I am to provide for twenty thousand men and their horses. I have no idea how many of those twenty thousand men are cavalry, of course, nor how much a horse eats per day, but that is a significant part of my burden. Yet you did not mention it.'

'I did not notice it. My apologies, Governor.'

'My point was not to upbraid you for neglecting horses, Fleckstein. It was to show that even when an intelligent man such as yourself has just read a document he may not be able to give an accurate summary of it. Without a document in evidence I cannot convict Kirschbaum.'

Fleckstein appeared flustered for the first time in my presence. Good — I was winning. 'Perhaps he has a draft among his papers.'

'A draft is not the published article. He may have had second thoughts.'

'I will enquire of the printer.'

'That is another question, Fleckstein. Why is the man who printed and published this document not before me?'

'He is a respectable citizen, Governor.'

'How can he be a respectable citizen if he is prepared to publish such a document as you assert was circulated? Or, alternatively, how can the document be so scurrilous if this paragon was prepared to print it? I cannot say that I understand this, Fleckstein.'

'No complaint was made against the printer, Governor.'

'Really? Then tell me more about this man Kirschbaum.'

'What is there to tell, Governor? He is a prolific pamphleteer and agitates for Moers being absorbed into Germany.'

'Have there been previous complaints against him?'

'Not exactly.'

'Is that not exactly yes, or not exactly no.'

'No.'

'So this is a first offence?'

'But a serious one, Governor.'

'If proven. But since I haven't seen a copy, I can't judge that.'

I sank back in my chair. In my time I had been given some very unpleasant tasks by William of Orange, but this topped them all (so far). I was manifestly unfitted for this job and I had no idea how to learn to do it better. On top of all this, I had not found a library anywhere and the local beer was not to my taste. I said a quick prayer for guidance.

Suddenly an idea came to me, an idea so brilliant that I could only assume that I was less of a sinner than I thought and the Almighty had decided to give me a hand.

'Let us suppose that you are right and the pamphlet was offensive to the Prince of Orange, Fleckstein,' I said. 'In a very short while he will be here at the head of his army. I will leave it to him to decide what punishment is appropriate. Of course, if a copy of the pamphlet is found I may reconsider my position.'

Fleckstein bowed to acknowledge my decision, or lack of a decision if you prefer, but made no attempt to leave.

'Was there something else, Fleckstein?' I asked, dreading the answer.

'Heribert Krul is outside, Governor. He craves an audience.'

'To what end?'

'He wishes to know when his wife will be returned to him as the law requires.'

I am not a vain or pompous man, but — [Van der Meer has twitched and knocked his inkpot over, and now I have forgotten what I was going to say. Read back those last few lines, Van der Meer, and try not to jerk about so much] — ah, yes, I am not a vain or pompous man, but I was not going to be told by a wife-beater where my duty lay.

'She will be returned when the legal processes are complete, Fleckstein.'

'Indeed so, Governor, but when shall I tell him that will be?'

I wanted to tell him it would be when Hell freezes over, but that might look like I was prejudging the case, so I had to find a better answer. 'If a woman wishes to enter a nunnery I could hardly divert her from her service to God to return her to her sinful life, could I?'

'I did not know that Alida Krul had expressed a desire for the religious life, Governor.'

'She hasn't. But I haven't asked her yet. I will do so at our next interview. Please explain that to Herr Krul. If he is difficult about it have him whipped.'

I don't know what possessed me to say that. It is contrary to everything I stand for, and I can only imagine that power was going to my head. However, having said it I could hardly retract it without damaging my image as a stern but just Governor.

Fleckstein shuddered a bit, but went out to give my message to Krul, and shortly afterwards I heard a door being slammed below me.

'Has he gone?' I asked.

'Herr Krul or Herr Fleckstein?' asked Biesma.

'Both.'

'Herr Krul is stomping across the courtyard, waving his fist in our general direction. Dear me, that is far too fine a hat to throw into the mud like that!'

'Close the door, Biesma, if you will.'

Biesma did so.

'What do you make of Fleckstein?' I asked. 'Is it only me who finds him insufferable?'

Biesma winced at the word. 'It is not my place…' he began.

'I asked you a question,' I reminded him.

'He is, perhaps, rather wedded to the old ways,' Biesma admitted. 'And no.'

'No? No what?'

'No, Governor, you are not the only man who finds him insufferable. But we must work with him. I think he would be a formidable enemy.'

I sighed. Biesma was right; but just at that moment I needed time and space to think. 'Get our cloaks,' I said. 'We're going out.'

'Where are we going?'

'To the Erlers' farm. I want to view the scene of the crime, and I want to do it now, before I have someone hanged on impulse.'

Despite my intentions and desires, when my carriage arrived at the farm, Fleckstein was in it. He saw us leaving and demanded that the driver stop until he had spoken to me; then, having ascertained our mission, declared that he would come too to offer his assistance. He also had the nerve to suggest that he could direct the driver, though the stout fellow had shown no sign of unfamiliarity with the route.

I was inclined to tell Fleckstein to boil his head, but Biesma lent over and whispered to me. 'Governor, is it wise to leave Fleckstein here unsupervised?'

'Ah. Good point,' I whispered back, then aloud I said, 'Herr Fleckstein, your assistance is always welcome. We'll wait while you get your cloak.'

Fleckstein disappeared, and I tried to remember the German for 'Drive on', but it had not come to me before the door opened and Fleckstein embedded himself in the seat alongside Biesma, who offered him a feeble smile of welcome.

I had overlooked telling Pringle where we were going, but he speedily detached half a dozen men on horseback and sent them after us to act as an escort. This I thought completely unnecessary, and I had just opened the window to tell the lieutenant that when a clod of earth smacked me in the face.

I was too much engaged in spitting out mud to say anything useful, but Fleckstein immediately shouted 'Stop the carriage!' and jumped out to demand that the soldiers seize the villain who had thrown it. He was fleet of foot, but a horse is faster, and in a few minutes he was being dragged before me and thrown to his knees on the ground.

The young lieutenant desperately wanted to do the right thing. 'Shall I cut off his hand, Governor?'

'Of course!' Fleckstein barked. 'Do you need to ask?'

'Was it his left hand or his right hand?' the lieutenant enquired. 'I didn't see it clearly and I wouldn't want to chop the wrong one off.'

'Don't do anything,' I finally managed to say.

The malefactor was a youth, perhaps sixteen years old, clad in a dark brown leather jerkin and thick woollen breeches.

'Lieutenant, you might remove the hatchet hanging from his belt,' I said, thanking God that he had thrown a handful of soil instead of the more lethal weapon readily to hand. 'Young man, why did you throw mud at me?'

'I wasn't throwing it at you,' he protested. 'Towards you, certainly, but there was nothing personal in it.'

'Nothing personal? Do you throw mud at everyone on this road?'

He looked at me as if I was the veriest idiot in Christendom. 'Not everyone, no. Only bigwigs in carriages.'

'Why?'

He shrugged. 'It's what you do, isn't it? There's us, and there's them. And you're one of them.'

'From where I'm standing, I'm one of us,' I replied.

'*Their* us, possibly, but not *our* us. If the ordinary workers of the world do not stand together against the oppression of the ruling classes, we'll be forever downtrodden.'

'And how does throwing clods at me help that struggle?'

'It's just a gesture of contempt and disgust at your easy life and how you have no concern for us.'

'Easy life! You should try doing my job for a day! You realise that I could have you punished?' I asked.

He gulped. 'Yes.'

'Then why did you do it?'

'I didn't think you'd catch me,' he answered. 'They never have before.'

Fleckstein was tutting. I could sense that if he had his way the lad would soon never need a whole pair of gloves again.

'What's your name?' I asked, as much to prolong the conversation and irritate Fleckstein as to gain the information.

'Paulus. Paulus Birmler.'

'Well, Paulus, what do you think I should do with you?'

'Sir?'

'I'm asking you how you think you should be punished. You do agree that your act merits punishment?'

He looked doubtful. 'I suppose so.'

'So I ask again, what should I do with you?'

Paulus turned his cap round and round in his hands as he thought. 'I think, Excellency, you should let me go.'

'Why?'

'Because then I would tell all my friends how fair and generous you are, and people would think well of you.'

'And stop throwing earth at my carriage?'

'Yes, Excellency.'

I turned his words over in my mind. You see, I do enjoy a good argument, and I had been missing them. This fellow was no student, but he could have given some of my undergraduates a run for their money when it came to constructing a response to my questioning. 'Very well. Lieutenant, give him his hatchet. Off you go, Paulus.'

'Really?'

'Yes, really. Don't forget to tell all your friends.'

He snatched up his hatchet, got to his feet and started running before I could change my mind. 'I will, Excellency!' he promised.

'If I may say so, that is excessively lenient,' Fleckstein protested. 'How can we maintain law and order if you let offenders off like that?'

'Your concern is noted, Fleckstein,' I replied. 'But he has put me in a good humour and the Lord Almighty knows nothing else here has done so.'

I climbed back into the carriage and found myself smiling as we trotted on.

CHAPTER TWELVE

The Erlers' farm was a depressing place. The only thing that distinguished it from the farms where I grew up was that there were hills in the distance, not a common sight in the Low Countries.

A rickety gate gave access to a small yard in which there were chicken coops. The farmhouse was a low building with a roof that was in need of some attention. Originally tiled, the broken tiles had been replaced with inexpert thatching. An angled plank tied to the roof deflected rainwater away from the door. The yard continued round the back of the house and it was here that Hubert Erler had been digging when he had been discovered.

'Who found him?' I asked.

'Their neighbour, a man called Pitten. He heard raised voices and came to see what had happened in case someone needed help.'

'I see. Let us ask Herr Pitten to join us. I should like to hear what he has to tell.'

A soldier was dispatched to fetch the witness and soon he shambled in front of us.

Herr Pitten was eighty years old if he was a day. What earthly use he would have been in the event of an emergency I could not say. To compound his other frailties, he was profoundly deaf.

'I am the Governor of Moers,' I bellowed at him.

'Very well, thank you, Your Excellency,' he replied.

Just at that moment the door to the farm opened and a young woman stepped out. She was armed with a knife. 'Who are you and what do you want here?' she demanded.

'I am Mercurius, Governor of Moers,' I replied. How good that sounded! 'And you are?'

She bobbed an inexpert curtsey. 'Anna Erler, if it please Your Excellency.'

'I have come to investigate the sad death of your parents,' I explained. 'I do not want to distress you by talking about unpleasant matters. Perhaps you should go inside.'

She nodded mutely.

'I will send for you before I leave,' I added.

Anna walked back into the house and I turned back to Pitten.

'That's the daughter, Anna,' he explained. 'And there's a brother, Hubert, who was digging here when I came round to see if I could help.'

'What did you hear?' I asked.

'What?' he yelled back. 'You'll have to speak up, I'm hard of hearing.'

'You came because you heard something. What did you hear?'

'I was back in the house beyond; well, not in the house as such, more in the yard, I suppose, for I was sitting on the step while my granddaughter was churning butter. "Did you hear that?" says she. "Hear what?" says I, for I'm hard of hearing, you see. "That hullabaloo next door," says she. "What hullabaloo?" says I. "It sounded like someone crying for help," says she. So I said to her to stay there, on account of her being halfway through churning and what with a baby on the way, her third, praise be to God, and let's hope this one lives longer than the others. And I went round to see what was to do.'

'Did you come by the road or over the back fence?' I asked.

'Eh?'

[Van der Meer has pointed out that this dialogue will become tedious to the reader if I describe all the repetitions and misunderstandings. No doubt he is right. I mention them here only to explain why it took the better part of an hour to get the essential facts from him, and the reader may suppose that it was one of the most difficult hours of my life.]

'Did you come that way, or that way?' I asked, pointing out each route in turn.

'By the road, Your Excellency. The pigsty is in the way if you try to go over the fence.'

'And did you see anyone else?'

'No, not a soul.'

'Is your granddaughter at home?'

'Yes, Your Excellency.'

'Then let us ask her if she can add anything to your account.'

We all trooped next door where a young woman was resting on a stool by the open kitchen door. I am no expert in these matters, but the size of the bump on her front suggested that we ought to ask our questions with all speed in case nature interrupted us.

When she saw us coming she attempted to stand respectfully.

'Please, mevrouw, sit,' I ordered, and introduced myself. 'Your grandfather says that you heard a noise next door on the day that the Erlers were murdered.'

'Yes, if it please Your Excellency. There were voices raised in anger.'

'Could you hear what was being said?'

She shook her head. 'Only that they were angry.'

'And how many voices did you hear?'

'I think three. Two men, and a woman.'

'Presumably the Erlers and their killer, Hubert,' Biesma interjected.

'And what did your grandfather say when he returned from investigating?'

'He said he'd found Hubert digging a grave and he could see the parents dead on the floor of the house.'

'And what did he do?'

'He said he must go at once to town to tell the Governor's office what he had seen. And that's what he did.'

'Wasn't he worried about leaving you here with a murderer next door?'

'Yes. He told me to bolt the door and stay within until he returned. I would know it was him for he would knock four times, in two pairs, thus: rap-rap, rap-rap.'

I turned to Fleckstein. 'Did Hubert Erler attempt to run while Pitten was walking to town? He must have had ample time, given Pitten's infirmity.'

'No, Governor, so far as we could make out he carried on burying his parents.'

'Isn't that curious?' I mused, but nobody answered. 'Was your husband at home at that time?' I asked the granddaughter.

'I don't know where he was. He went off looking for work.'

'Seven months ago,' Pitten chipped in. 'Bastard. Begging your pardon, Excellency.'

I thanked the young woman, wished her well in her travails, and assured her of my prayers for a safe delivery of a healthy child, and we returned to the Erlers' house. For some reason old Pitten seemed to think he was still needed and tagged along too.

Anna Erler looked pale and tired; no wonder, for she was trying to keep the farmstead going single-handedly while Hubert was in prison. She had been crying, betrayed by the redness of her eyes and the crumpled kerchief gripped tightly in her hand.

I glanced about the kitchen. It was generally clean and tidy, with the heel of a loaf on the table. It was days old.

'When did you last eat?' I asked her.

'I'm not hungry,' she replied.

'That isn't what I asked.'

She began to cry again. 'I don't know. Some days ago. The day before yesterday, perhaps.'

'Is there anything here to eat?'

'I'm sorry. I should have offered you something,' she said, rising from her seat in some confusion.

'No, that's not my point,' I assured her. 'I see nothing that you could eat. I fear that you are neglecting yourself.'

'What's the point in living?' she wailed. 'My parents are dead, my brother like to follow, and I am alone in the world. I cannot manage the farm by myself. I would be better off dead.'

'You must put such thoughts aside,' I directed her sternly. 'Our lives are sacred.'

'Yet you will take Hubert's,' she snapped back.

'That is yet to be decided,' I told her. 'And since he will not defend himself, it is not easy to find any mitigating circumstances for what he has done. Can you throw any light on this?'

She shook her head violently. 'I have asked myself again and again why he has done this,' she replied. 'He will not let me visit him and sent a message saying that he does not want to speak to me. No doubt he is protecting me by preparing me for the time when he is not here, but it is painful.'

'And there was nothing beforehand that might suggest a reason for his actions?'

'Nothing. We were a very happy family. He loved our parents and they loved him.'

There seemed no more to be said.

'What will become of you now?' I asked.

'My parents had arranged a marriage for me with Martin Laut, but I don't know if he will still want me, given the notoriety of my family name.'

'Have you spoken to Herr Laut about it?'

'No. I thought it would look forward of me. I left it to him to make the first move.'

'And he hasn't?'

'I haven't seen him since before all this happened. And I thought he was really keen to marry me. What a fool I am!'

'Perhaps he doesn't know what he could say to you,' I suggested.

'Sometimes it's difficult to find the right words when someone has had something bad in their life, I understand that. But that doesn't excuse silence. Better to say something than say nothing.'

The young can be remarkably wise sometimes. Not my undergraduates, obviously, but there are occasional shining exceptions to that rule. It is important to say something to the bereaved, however inadequate; not to do so might suggest that you thought their loss unworthy of comment.

I bowed my thanks to her and walked a few steps away so that she would not hear my next question to Fleckstein. 'What happened to the bodies?'

'The bodies, Governor? Why, they are here!'

'Here?'

'Yes. By the time our men arrived, Erler had buried his parents and it seemed disrespectful to move them.'

'But surely this is not consecrated ground.'

'No, but our first thought was to secure Erler and take him to await justice.'

'So nobody has examined the bodies?'

Fleckstein appeared confused. 'I can assure you that they were definitely dead, Governor.'

'That is not what I meant. No surgeon viewed the corpses to mark their injuries, and give an opinion on the cause and time of death?'

'No, Governor. We knew when they had died, and we knew how they had died from Herr Pitten's testimony.'

'This is most unsatisfactory, Fleckstein. It flies in the face of all established procedure in such matters.'

'You must forgive us, Governor. We do not have as many murders as you clearly do in Leiden.'

I think he was being sarcastic, but you never know with these people. A lot of Germans sound sarcastic even when they aren't. 'We do not have many murders in Leiden, Fleckstein. That is because the criminal classes know their villainy will be properly investigated and they will be discovered.'

That told him. Actually, it was true. There are not many murders in Leiden compared with, say, Oxford or Glasgow, Padua or Paris. But we do have a lot of experience of fishing dead drunks out of canals. Only last year one of my students fell off a bridge while drunk and landed on a barge. He didn't even have the brains to fall in a canal properly.

There seemed only one possible course of action. 'We must exhume them, Fleckstein.'

'Exhume them? Surely the dead should lie undisturbed?'

'Ordinarily, yes; but the Erlers have been denied a Christian burial.'

'A minister said prayers over their grave.'

'How do we know they are even in there, Fleckstein?'

'Well, where else would they be?' he stuttered.

'I want to see the bodies,' I insisted. To be honest, I definitely didn't. I don't like corpses at the best of times and these had been in the earth some weeks. But I know my duty. 'And I want them examined by a competent doctor. You do have a competent doctor, I take it?'

'Oh, yes, Governor. Probably.'

'I don't want the daughter to see this. Is there anywhere she can be lodged for the time being?'

'I can't think of anywhere suitable.'

'Then lodge her in the castle.'

'Governor, that would be most improper! People will talk.'

'Not with me, of course,' I added quickly. That construction had not occurred to me, I admit. 'But there must be a room somewhere in the castle that she could have?'

Biesma came to the rescue. 'I will find her quarters with the kitchen maids, Governor.'

'Excellent. Thank you, Biesma. You may take my carriage to convey her to the castle. Fleckstein, please go too and come back with it and some men with spades and two coffins. Some lanterns would be helpful too, in case we cannot complete the task by nightfall.'

The carriage departed with its passengers. It had taken Anna Erler a depressingly short time to pack her clothes, since she had very few. Pitten remained beside me at my request, and one of the soldiers translated for me.

'When you saw Hubert Erler burying the bodies, where were they lying?' I asked him.

'I could only see their legs at first. Each was lying in the kitchen, Frau Erler nearer the door with her head to the right and her feet to the left, and Herr Erler was on the other side of the table, the same. Head right, feet left. Not quite so much sideways across the room, though.'

'And did you see their wounds?'

'I pushed the door open, Excellency, to see what had befallen them. They were both quite dead, I can assure you. Both had been stabbed a few times.'

'And were they dressed as you usually saw them?'

'They didn't have outdoor clothes or boots on. They must have been inside for a time. Herr Erler was much as he usually was, except his doublet was buttoned. Frau Erler — well, forgive me, Governor — her skirts were up a bit near her knees, the poor woman. She'd have been so ashamed if she'd known. She was always very proper, you see. I pulled them down for her. And she looked so shocked. His face was like he'd fallen asleep. She was a bit wild-eyed, I'd have said, as if she didn't understand what was happening. Well, you don't expect your own son to kill you, do you?'

No, you don't, I thought. *So why did he?*

Fleckstein returned with my carriage, and shortly afterwards a cart arrived with half a dozen men, each carrying a spade. They had to walk alongside because the cart bore a pair of cheap coffins. The poorer classes are usually buried without coffins, just in a winding-sheet, but I expected that this would not prove satisfactory for bodies that must already have begun to decompose.

In an unexpected display of thoughtfulness Fleckstein had also brought some kerchiefs and a basket of herbs. We each grabbed a handful and wrapped them in a ball that we could hold under our noses during the exhumation or, in my case, over my eyes if it all became too much.

It was quite clear where the soil had been disturbed by Hubert Erler, so I set the men to work, asking them to dig from the edges towards the centre, and to be mindful of the delicacy of what might lie underneath. To their credit, they soon understood what was needed and worked carefully and methodically, taking off just a hand's-width of soil at a time, by which means a male hand was soon exposed. One of the men had a small trowel with which he managed to outline the shape of Herr Erler's body, and soon after Frau Erler's apron could be seen, so he did the same for her.

It took a couple of hours, but before long we were looking at a couple lying side by side in a relatively shallow grave.

As I looked at them, Herr Erler was to the left, his wife to the right. Both were fully dressed. Rather incongruously Herr Erler had his woollen hat over his face. The bodies were dirty and Frau Erler's mouth must have been open, so a quantity of soil had fallen in. Their garments were in good condition and a number of stab wounds could be seen on each. This was not the place to make a record of that; rather, I wanted to glean as much information as I could from the grave.

'Fleckstein, how long would it take to dig a grave of this size?' I asked.

'I have absolutely no idea, Governor. I am unaccustomed to manual labour.'

That may well have been true, but he did not need to sound quite so dismissive of the idea.

I glanced around me and saw Herr Pitten loitering behind me under a tree. 'Herr Pitten,' I bellowed, 'how long would it take a man to dig such a grave?'

Pitten removed his cap. Whether this was out of respect, because it helped him think without overheating his brain, or his scalp was itchy, I cannot say.

'Well, let me see, now. 'Tis twice as wide as a normal grave, so say it's two graves. But it's only about half as deep. But this is well-trodden earth, quite compacted I'd say. 'Twouldn't be easy digging, even for a fit lad like Hubert. But then we had quite a bit of rain before, so the soil might have been softened, you wouldn't want to dig this in January…' He wittered on like this for a couple of minutes before finally drawing all his ruminations to a conclusion. 'I don't know.'

'Perhaps I should set you to digging one like it, then we could time you,' I snapped.

'But I'm coming to think it would have been the best part of an afternoon, if it please Your Excellency,' he quickly added.

I thanked him — for what, I was not too sure — and returned to Fleckstein. 'What time did they arrest Hubert Erler?'

'I cannot be sure, Governor, but it was growing dark when Pitten arrived at the castle, and the men carried lanterns to come out here.'

'And what exactly was Hubert doing when the men arrived?'

Fleckstein called to the man with the trowel. 'Greck, the Governor is asking what Hubert Erler was doing when you got here.'

Greck walked towards me, swiftly removing his cap and holding it in front of him as if he expected me to kick him in the groin and thought it might protect him somewhat. 'He was chucking soil in the pigsty, Your Governorship.'

'The soil from the grave?' I enquired.

'I think it must have been. There was no mound, because that would have given away what he had been about. And to be honest, if old Pitten hadn't told us what we were looking for, we'd barely have seen the grave, seeing as it was coming on dark by then.'

'The grave was fully dug, then?'

'Dug, aye, and filled in again.'

'Thank you, Greck.'

Something was puzzling me, something not quite right about the story I was being given. Yet I could not have told you what it was. And the irritating thing was that if someone had constructed a faulty syllogism, or misquoted Thomas Aquinas, I'd have been in my element. I should have pounced and ripped their argument to pieces on the spot; but I was out of my depth in a world where men dig holes to bury their dead parents and conceal the evil that they have done.

But how could Hubert have ever hoped to get away with it? Sooner or later someone would notice that his parents were not around. Pitten lived less than a field's-length away and obviously knew them well; he had been visibly moved when their bodies were unearthed. And long before that Anna would return from her visit and it would make for an awkward conversation around the supper table.

'*Would you like some more broth, Hubert? By the way, any idea where Ma and Pa have got to?*'

'*Oh, yes, I was meaning to mention that. I stabbed them both to death and buried them in the back yard earlier.*'

It didn't seem very likely, put like that.

CHAPTER THIRTEEN

There are people who can achieve a lot because anyone they meet immediately recognises them as essentially good. Biesma was such a man.

It seemed that having arrived at the castle he had sought out the housekeeper and explained why Anna Erler was there. Despite her many duties the housekeeper had taken her in hand and suggested that her hair should be washed and brushed because any woman feels better when her hair is well dressed, during which time some soup had been warmed and fresh bread taken from the oven. Biesma sat opposite Anna and while he took nothing himself he gently coaxed her to eat a little something. It was at the kitchen table that I found her on my return.

'No, do not stop,' I insisted. 'My questions will wait. I only wanted to let you know that we have retrieved your parents' bodies and we will take them for cleaning and preparation for burial.'

'I should do that,' she blurted out, half-rising from the table before Biesma gently pulled at her elbow and caused her to sit once more.

'I don't think they are fit for a young lady just now, but when we have examined them they will be cleaned and I will send for you so you can say farewell to them.'

Whether their coffins would be open or closed would depend on the extent to which we could make the corpses look half normal. Certainly we would have to find a way of keeping Frau Erler's mouth closed. Until they were cleaned it was not easy to determine how ghastly they looked.

I was tempted to ask for a bowl of soup myself, firstly because it looked good and, more importantly, because I was finding the life of a governor exceedingly solitary. I had had many wild notions of feasting in merry company with all those who worked in the castle, presiding at a great board and occasionally lobbing a chicken leg towards some favoured underling. Not that feasting is my favoured behaviour, you understand, but I thought that it might be expected of me.

In fact, I usually ate alone. Occasionally Pringle would join me, but he was too busy at the moment fleecing the inhabitants of Moers of anything that the army might need which, to judge from the letters of complaint I was receiving, included all the apples in town, a large number of boots and the occasional cart. Biesma did not think it proper to share a table with his master, and while Fleckstein did, I did not think it proper to share a table with anyone like Fleckstein. As for that valet Tap, I had not seen him for a day or two and had no idea what use a personal servant was who did not stay close to my person. Admittedly my linen was all clean and folded, so the fellow had clearly been doing something to earn whatever it was he was being paid, but the opportunity to have a word or two with him would have been good.

I wearily tramped to my presence chamber to see what had been happening while I had been at the farm and found my passage through the corridor blocked by a crowd of supplicants. One claimed to have had twenty pigs taken without a receipt by Pringle's men, which shocked me a great deal, until another man declared that the blackguard did not have twenty pigs in the first place and that this was a clear attempt to defraud the public purse; in contrast to which his own demand for recompense for two barrels of Rhine wine was entirely justified. These, it appeared, had not been removed by Pringle's men, but consumed on the spot as they went about their business, sequestrating property being thirsty work. Since Biesma was in the kitchen I directed them all to leave their claims with Fleckstein, who looked at me with the nearest thing to an evil eye I had ever encountered. They followed him, leaving just one man sitting on a bench against the wall.

'And what do you want?' I snapped, rather unkindly.

'If it please Your Excellency, I'd like my daughters back.'

'Daughters? How many daughters?'

'Two, Your Excellency. There's Griselda, and there's Brida. Lovely girls, though I say so myself.'

'And where are they now?'

'Gone with the army. They've been debauched, most likely.'

This sort of thing made my blood boil. Soldiers are no respecters of women and the prospect of presiding over a county full of ruined girls did not appeal to me. I summoned a nearby guard. 'Find Captain Pringle and demand that he attends upon me immediately. I don't care what he's doing. I want him in my office!'

I took the supplicant's name and promised him that I would investigate the matter personally, and that if liberties had been taken with his daughters the men responsible would pay dearly for their wickedness.

'I was hoping for compensation,' he moaned. 'Hanging them is no use to me.'

I had not actually considered what I was going to do with them, but hanging had not come into it. I was thinking more of a sharp dressing-down involving liberal use of sarcasm, but I could see that an outraged father might not think that this met the case.

'Leave it to me, Herr Eberlin, and I will find out what has happened to your daughters. Come back tomorrow evening and we'll talk some more.'

Eberlin thanked me profusely for having agreed to take up his cause, and soon I was alone in my office looking at a pile of papers. Given my low mood the arrival of Fleckstein was extremely unwelcome.

'Have they gone?' he whispered.

'Were you hiding from them?' I accused him.

'Not at all. I merely wanted to avoid interrupting any confidential conversation you might be having.'

'You're my confidential secretary, Fleckstein. I don't have anything confidential from you.'

Fleckstein brightened at once, and I'll swear he grew a few inches in height. 'It is kind of you to say so,' he began.

'These papers…' I muttered.

'Just so. If you will sign here, here and here,' he continued, pointing to the first sheet.

'You should know by now that I never sign anything that I have not read.'

'Of course, Governor. Perish the thought. Shall I leave you for a couple of hours?'

'I have a splitting headache already, Fleckstein. Read them to me.'

If I had to sit through them I did not see why he should escape. As it was, I was so bewildered by all the instances of "whereas", "heretofore", "notwithstanding" and "our High and Mighty Prince" in the first document that I snatched it back off him because I could not follow it. 'If I understand correctly, this is a permit to hold a fair.'

'Indeed, Governor.'

'Which has been held every year since time immemorial.'

'Just so, Governor.'

'Which means…?'

'Well, nobody knows exactly when it started.'

'Could you give me an approximation?'

Fleckstein stroked his chin. 'It is mentioned in a charter of 1173, I believe.'

'So someone has asked permission to do what has been done every year for over five hundred years?'

'Not every year, Governor. Plague, famine and war have intervened.'

'Don't nitpick, Fleckstein. Over five hundred years.'

'But without the Governor's permission it would not be legal. They must ask every year.'

I took a quill and dipped it in my inkhorn before scratching out a phrase and inserting one of my own. 'There! They may hold their wretched fair for the next five years without asking again.'

'Forgive me, Governor, but that is not how things have been done here.'

'No,' I conceded, 'perhaps not, but it is how they are going to be done now. I am waging war on unnecessary paperwork, Fleckstein.'

I thought he was going to faint. He staggered momentarily and steadied himself against the corner of my table. Mind you, I had surprised myself too. Never before had I thought that there was too much paper in the world.

I wanted to put this aside and concentrate on the Erlers' murders, but I did not want to give the impression that I was neglecting my duties. 'I'm tired, Fleckstein. Bring the rest to me tomorrow, if you will. I am going to the chapel to pray.' A horrible thought struck me. 'You do have a chapel, I suppose?'

'Certainly. Would you like the Catholic fripperies within destroyed?'

'Destroyed?'

'As a Leiden man you are sure to be a fervent devotee of the Reformed faith, Governor.'

'Ah, yes. Of course. But I am not a zealot. Leave things be, and I shall turn a blind eye to them. After all, I am here but for a season, and the next Governor may differ in religion from me.'

'Unlikely, Governor. The Prince always picks Reformed men.'

'Then why are the statues still here?'

Fleckstein had the grace to look embarrassed. 'The previous Governor pawned them. When he was dismissed we retrieved them.'

Previously I had prayed in my room and after one look at the chapel I decided I should probably revert back to that. The chapel was filthy. I doubt it had been dusted for many years; I might have said centuries, except that I recognised a painting on the wall as a poor copy of a famous fresco by Leonardo depicting the Last Supper. The chapel was very small, and the artist had chosen not to alter the scale of the original, but instead had lopped three apostles off each end to give the impression that only half of the Twelve turned up to the Last Supper. Admittedly I have not seen Leonardo's original, but I was fairly sure that he painted a full set of apostles in his.

I knelt in prayer, though in truth I just wanted some peace to think, and a bit of help from the Almighty to solve these crimes would not come amiss either. I was not hopeful. God had not offered much help in solving my previous cases, so I saw no reason why he would start now.

I closed my eyes and prayed fervently for assistance in carrying out my duties. Surely God would not ignore my prayer? I had been a faithful servant of his — well, relatively faithful — for many years and I had not asked for much in that time, apart from long life, comfort, the miraculous appearance of a dagger in my hand to defend myself, the smiting of an opponent or two and some help with solving mysteries, that is. But as I knelt there I suddenly became aware of a voice saying, 'What is it you want of me?'

My eyes flew open in surprise. I fixed them on a figure of Christ on the cross on the altar but Our Lord's lips did not seem to be moving. Then I remembered that it was unlikely that Almighty God had a Scottish accent, and turned to find Pringle standing behind me, his hat politely tucked under his arm.

'Forgive me,' I said. 'I was deep in prayer.'

'So it seemed,' remarked Pringle drily. 'It is as well that I had no murderous intent, for I could have slit your throat easily then.'

He seemed to expect gratitude for his forbearance, whereas now that I had recalled why I had sent for him, I intended to subject him to a tirade of some severity. 'I have had complaints,' I told him, 'about the army.'

'Of course, Governor. I would be surprised if you had not.'

'You're not concerned?'

'I am concerned that you are concerned, but without more specific information I do not know how concerned I ought to be. What exactly are they complaining about?'

'The level of your depredations for one. Is it really necessary to requisition so much for your soldiers' use?'

'I don't know,' Pringle answered. 'The length of a war is unpredictable. We don't usually agree with the enemy how long it is going to last, you see.'

'But we're not equipping the army for the whole war. Our orders only ask us to collect enough for the journey into France.'

'Shh, Governor! Our destination is a secret!'

'I have little patience with this. Anyone with half a brain would realise that if an army is being gathered in Nijmegen and marched to Moers it can only be heading in one direction.'

'That is why we have tried not to draw attention to the mustering of the army at Nijmegen.'

I gasped at the effrontery of this suggestion. 'How can anyone not notice an army on their doorstep? The citizens of Moers have certainly noticed one!'

'With respect, Governor, what you or the citizens of Moers see is immaterial. All that matters is that our plans are effected quickly before King Louis has time to react. Even if spies reported our arrival in Nijmegen to him, it will take him time to gather his troops; but not much time, which is why I am driving as hard as I can. We must be on the move within a day or two. It would be a great help if you would publicly call now for further troops to quell the disorder here as the Stadhouder instructed.'

'Disorder? What disorder?'

'The riots caused by the army seizing food.'

'But there are no riots.'

'You know that, and I know that, but the Stadhouder is far off and will believe what his Governor tells him. As you know, he wants a pretext to move more troops here.'

'I'm not acquiescing in a lie, Pringle. There is no rioting.'

Pringle thought for a moment. 'I could start a riot if it helps your conscience.'

'No!'

'Just a wee one. Nobody needs to get seriously hurt.'

'No! As Governor my prime concern is the welfare of the people I govern.'

'What a novel approach. I don't think I've ever heard that from a Governor before.'

'Pringle, you are impossibly cynical.'

'Maybe, but if I may speak freely, Governor, you are impossibly naïve. With or without your co-operation the Stadhouder will move his troops. Doing so under cover of a request from his Governor would make him look better, that's all. And I'm sure neither of us wants to make the Stadhouder look bad.'

Put like that, I was caught in an impossible position. If I did not request more troops William might proceed with too few, be defeated, and our country would suffer. I certainly would if William caught up with me. I tried to calculate how far I would have to go to get out of his reach. I had heard that Lithuania is pretty at that time of year. 'I'll write tonight,' I conceded.

'Thank you, Governor. I knew you'd see sense.'

'But now you need to do something for me. I've had a man here complaining that your men have abducted his daughters.'

'Nonsense.'

'How can you be so sure?'

'My lads do not abduct young women. But we are troubled by camp followers, here as everywhere else.'

'Camp followers? What are they?'

'Prostitutes who follow the army to supply the soldiers' baser needs. And do their laundry, I suppose.'

'These women are not prostitutes.'

'Not yet. But they soon will be if they hang around the army long enough.'

'Pringle, I want the men who did this rooted out and punished with the utmost severity.'

Pringle stroked his chin. 'Governor, I'll root them out. But as for punishment, consider what the Stadhouder would think. He needs every man he can get. What do you suppose he'll say when he hears you've been having good fighting men strung up?'

'I — er — that is, discipline must be maintained,' I stammered. 'We are a Christian army.'

'There's no such thing, Governor. An army is composed, for the most part, of savages. They don't trouble themselves with philosophical concerns.'

'I don't need them hanged. I just want them punished. I want their colleagues to know that this will not be tolerated. I want to ensure that this does not happen again.'

Pringle appeared pained by my insistence. 'Tell you what. If I can find out who did it, I'll have them publicly emasculated. That should do the trick, and they'll be able to fight again after a few days' recuperation. How's that?'

I realise that many ill-informed people doubt the manliness of university lecturers and make disparaging comments about us. It is true that we are not customarily exceptionally muscular, but it takes a certain hardiness and dedication to sit still in a library for a day, often without taking food. Be that as it may, I admit that if I were emasculated I doubt that I would be turning over the pages of heavy books for quite a few weeks, and I very much doubted that soldiers, even the most doltish ones, would be back fighting after a few days; though I suppose a gelded soldier might fight with extra vigour, having nothing much to look forward to after the battle.

'Pringle, if you restore the women unscathed to their father and there's no harm done, you may punish or refrain from chastisement as you please.'

Pringle brightened considerably and took the women's names. He fished in his wallet for a suitable coin or two and bowed his agreement. 'Best to find the money in the light. I wouldn't want to hand it out in the dark and find I'd given good gold away.'

'You're proposing to reward them?'

'No, I'm proposing to reward any men who bring me the women unharmed. A couple of guilders apiece should suffice.'

'That's not a lot,' I protested.

'No, but it's money *now*. Some of these fellows won't live to draw their next pay so they'd rather have ready money now. By your leave, Governor.'

He bowed so low I doubted whether he would be able to right himself without something to lean on, but somehow he did, and I was left with my papers, my headache and my prayers.

Oh, and that flask of wine I had vowed not to drink from every time I had a bad day.

CHAPTER FOURTEEN

I understand that there are people who delight to hear the cock crow, leap from their beds giving praises to God for another day and wash and dress themselves with a song in their hearts. I have never been one such.

I like to say my morning prayers in a horizontal attitude, preferably with a warm blanket over me, and it is not a good thing to speak to me until I have had something to eat and drink; and as I age I become ever more fixed in this opinion, and would happily lie abed until noon if I had a good book to read.

This was prevented by the arrival of Tap bearing my shaving water, who evidently expected me to do something with it, since he set it on a stand and stropped my razor with gusto before offering it to me.

'Thank you,' I said through gritted teeth, wondering if it would be churlish to use the proffered razor on his thick little neck.

'I'll shave you if you like, Master,' he said, far too cheerfully for that time in the morning.

'Thank you, I can manage,' I replied. I am very fussy who I allow near my throat with an open razor, and I had not known Tap long enough to feel comfortable adding him to that very short list.

The blackguard made to leave me, but I stopped him with a command. 'Where have you been these last few days, Tap?'

'Oh, I understood you didn't need me.'

'Didn't need you? Who told you that?'

'Captain Pringle. He said he had a little job for me and you wouldn't miss me.'

'And what exactly was this little job, Tap?'

He looked uncomfortable and picked at the hem of his jerkin. 'The Captain said it was highly confidential, Governor.'

'Perhaps. But you can tell me. I am, after all, the source of all authority in this county.'

'I ought to ask the Captain…'

'With the power of life and death over all men…'

'Nevertheless, I really ought…'

'And complete control of the public purse.'

Tap surrendered. 'He desired me to take a message for him.'

'To whom?'

'To the Stadhouder, Governor.'

'You've been to The Hague and back?'

'No, Governor. The Stadhouder is near Nijmegen with his army.'

'I see. You didn't think to share this information with me?'

'It's not for me to say where the Stadhouder is, Governor. I thought you knew.'

'Tap, I am discovering that I know next to nothing about what is going on here, and that is not a healthy position to be in. From now on it is your job to see that I know everything. Do you understand?'

'Yes, Gov— Would you mind not waving your razor near my head, Master?'

I had not noticed that I was doing so. It just shows how vexed I was feeling. 'I am sorry. There, I've put it down. Now, what did the message say?'

Tap was indignant. 'It was a sealed letter! I wouldn't dream of betraying a confidence like that!'

I picked up my razor again.

'It was confirming that you'd collected all the stores the army needed and that the Stadhouder could now bring his army down to Moers,' he screeched, holding his hand across his neck just in case I became overexcited.

'Was there anything else?'

'He said what a good job you were doing and it was a pleasure to work with you.'

'Did he now?' I commented, a certain amount of suspicion in my voice.

'He did. More or less.'

'More or less?'

'I cannot remember the exact words, Governor, but that was his drift.'

'Tap, Pringle selected you for this job personally. He is not a fool, and he clearly prizes your gifts as a spy. Among which, undoubtedly, is the ability to remember long and complex messages precisely, so try harder before I lose what remains of my temper.'

This encouragement spurred Tap to new efforts and he recited the contents of the letter without hesitation or other difficulty. It was as he said, with the added snippets that Pringle looked forward to giving the French a well-deserved bloody nose and he thought that I had done so well here that I ought to be installed as Governor on a permanent basis. And I had thought that we were friends!

'Did the Stadhouder give you a reply to bring back?'

'Not a written one, Governor. He told me to tell Captain Pringle that he would hear from him either tonight or tomorrow morning.'

Presumably that would be confirmation that his troops were on the march, so it would not be long now before William arrived and I could remind him that my acceptance of this poisoned chalice was meant to be a temporary arrangement though, truth to tell, I wanted to stay long enough to get to the bottom of Hubert Erler's odd behaviour and to see Alida Krul's safety assured, even if I had no idea how to achieve that.

I dismissed Tap who left the room at a sprint in case I changed my mind, dressed myself with care so as to make the most imposing figure I could, complete with the chain of office, even though I was convinced that its weight was reducing my height by a thumb's-breadth every day, and marched downstairs to have a few things out with Pringle.

I am sure that I need not add that the villain was nowhere to be found. On questioning, the sentries at the gates of the town vaguely remembered that he might have gone out shortly before dawn to review his troops who were, for the most part, camped outside the gates, although even my unmilitary eyes could see that the army was loafing around on the grass in a most unsoldierly way such as they would never have dared if Pringle had been around.

The time had come for decisive action. 'Open the gates!' I ordered.

'Nobody is allowed in without the password, Governor.'

'Nobody is coming in. I am going out.'

'Right. Well, have you got the password?'

'I don't need a password!' I yelled. 'I am the Governor. I set the passwords.'

'Right, Just a minute then.'

They unbolted the large gates and threw them back.

'We keep them locked to keep the army out,' the guard explained.

'That is why I am going out to them. Kindly point me towards Lieutenant Schoenmaker.'

'I don't know him, Governor. We're Moers men, not the army.'

'Well, who looks like an officer there?'

The guards put their heads together. 'Him on the black horse with the big plume on his hat. He'll be an officer, I reckon.'

I stomped down the hill towards the man in question, and was gratified to observe a lot of bowing and fawning over me as I did so. Not that I enjoy that kind of thing, but it showed that people recognised the authority I had been temporarily given.

Seeing me on foot the officer sprang from his horse and saluted.

'You are…?' I said.

'Captain Johann van Teylingen,' he replied, saluting again.

'Good morning, Captain. I was looking for Captain Pringle. Do you know where he is?'

'I do not, Governor. I have not seen him since last night. I could make enquiries if you wish. However, my best guess is that he has gone ahead along the road we expect to follow very soon.'

'But he will be back?'

'Undoubtedly. Unless he has been ambushed, of course, but we have no reason to expect that.'

Can one expect an ambush? Logically that seemed an incoherent proposition, the very essence of an ambush being that it is not expected, but this was not the time for such by-play. 'He undertook to find two young women for me.'

'We have plenty to choose from, Governor. What type were you looking for?'

I could feel myself reddening despite my best efforts. 'You misunderstand me. These are a particular pair of young ladies whose father is concerned about their disappearance from home.'

I could see Van Teylingen constructing a story behind his eyes. Ordinarily he would not have troubled himself over a couple of errant young women, but if their father was influential enough to persuade a Governor to take up their case, then there was a possibility that he was a man of honour and this could end in a duel if not resolved satisfactorily. Little did he know that their father was an insignificant little fellow with poor eyesight, but that, of course, did not diminish his right to justice.

'Do you know their names, Governor?'

'Griselda and Brida Eberlin.'

'I will make enquiries and bring them to you personally.'

'I would be grateful, Captain.'

'Unless you want to look yourself. Wisman,' he called to a nearby fellow on a fine chestnut horse, 'lend your horse to the Governor, if you will. We'll return it presently.'

Wisman looked unhappy but dutifully jumped down from his mount and led it over to me.

Horses and I do not get on. In my presence they tend to forget the primary purpose of a horse, to move forward as commanded, and become static objects, except when walking backwards. I would gladly have foregone this torture, except that I sensed that it was in some measure a test of my earnestness in finding these young women. Thus I grasped the reins in my hand and grabbed the pommel of the saddle to lever myself up. Given the added weight of my chain, this proved extremely difficult, and I might be hanging off the side of the horse still if Wisman had not grabbed my feet and shoved me upwards. I managed to swing one leg over as I went and was soon sitting upright, albeit facing the wrong end of the animal, but I swiftly corrected this and I think the manoeuvre went off without drawing attention to my error.

We began walking through the soldiers towards a circle of carts further down the hill, when suddenly Van Teylingen spurred his beast on and it broke into a canter. I can manage to walk a horse, and have occasionally persuaded one to trot, but a canter was not something I relished, and I should have been content with a leisurely walk had it not been for Wisman who gave the horse a slap on the rump. I felt it myself, so goodness knows what the horse felt, but it took off at speed and I grabbed reins, mane and pommel and squeezed with both knees to stay on the animal. It appeared to know that it had to follow Van Teylingen, and after what seemed an hour but can only have been a couple of minutes the two creatures came to a halt by the carts. Van Teylingen walked his horse between two and I followed.

The circle of carts concealed signs of the greatest debauchery and laxity. Women with loose hair and half-open chemises abounded. One was openly washing her upper half. A soldier with his breeches round his knees was servicing a woman from behind as if they were brute beasts in a field (which, I suppose, they were).

'Griselda! Brida!' Van Teylingen shouted. I hoped very fervently that the woman bent over the cart end was not going to respond to these calls.

There was a fire going over which a pot hung, and one of the women tending it walked towards us, joined after a moment by another woman who had been brushing an officer's uniform.

'You're going back to your father,' Van Teylingen told them. They made as if to escape but the other women grabbed them. They did not want any trouble at their door. 'Now, one of you on each horse. Bring your bags if you have them.'

The larger one, whom I took to be Griselda, mounted in front of Van Teylingen, who tossed a few coppers towards the women who had detained them. Meanwhile Brida was attempting to mount beside me, but being shorter she could not reach. I leaned down to help her and she nearly pulled me off by tugging on my arm, but fortunately a couple of sturdy fellows lifted her bodily and placed her in front of me in a side-saddle posture. This necessitated my sliding back in the saddle so that her hip nestled against the pommel, and I was obliged to place an arm about her waist which discomfited me exceedingly.

Van Teylingen brushed aside the sentries who attempted to challenge him for the password, using a few words which were certainly not suitable as passwords, and deposited Griselda in the custody of a castle guard before jumping down to receive Brida from me. By judicious use of the castle steps I managed to dismount without making a complete fool of myself and thanked Van Teylingen, who bowed once more and then sprang into the saddle as if it were the easiest thing in the world.

Biesma came running in a most unseemly fashion. 'Governor, we've been looking for you. The surgeon is here.'

'Surgeon? What surgeon?'

Biesma lowered his voice. 'The surgeon who is to conduct the examination.'

His voice was low, but not so low that the women did not hear him.

'We are virgins still!' Brida insisted. 'There is no need for an examination.'

'I am delighted to hear it,' I answered, thinking that it were no bad thing if they continued under the misapprehension that the examination was planned for them rather than the Erlers' corpses. I told soldiers to take them to some lockable chamber and guard them there while I allowed Biesma to conduct me to an upper room where the surgeon was waiting.

'I thought it best to have the bodies moved here,' he explained, 'where the light is much better.'

The surgeon was waiting patiently, or as patiently as eminent surgeons ever wait. He had laid out his instruments and was peering into each of the bodies' faces in turn before he finally deigned to notice me.

'Governor! I am Dr Ruprecht Lippert. I will not offer you my hand because I have just washed them.'

He spoke to me in Latin, which was quite a relief. I rejoiced to be in the company of an educated man again, and relieved not to be straining my ears trying to decipher some barbarous German dialect.

'I have already observed these people closely and there appear to be no wounds to the face. I therefore propose to wipe off the dirt to see what we find.'

He did not wait for my permission but began carefully swabbing Herr Erler's skin. Lippert was an energetic, busy man, spare of frame, with long arms accentuated by his turned-back sleeves. He wore his black hair cut short, without a wig, was clean-shaven, perhaps somewhat taller than the average, with a ready smile. I immediately liked and trusted him, which is strange because I reached this conclusion based on hardly any evidence.

He rolled Frau Erler onto her stomach. 'Let us see if any of this earth falls from her orifices.'

It took me a moment to realise that he meant her nostrils and mouth.

Returning to Herr Erler, he took a piece of charcoal and quickly sketched an outline of the body. Grasping a length of cord he offered the loose end to me. 'Would you mind, Governor? Just hold it at the top of his head.'

He used the other end to mark the man's feet, held it against a measuring stick and calculated his height, which he noted on his drawing. He then repeated the act around Erler's waist. 'Rather heavier than he used to be, I fancy. Does he have a son?'

'He does,' I replied, 'who is suspected of killing him.'

'Clearly the son is now working on the farm with him and that has reduced the amount of heavy work that he was doing, so he has gained weight. Observe that the rope holding up his breeches is now tied further round than used to be the case.'

This was all quite impressive, if nothing to the point.

'Could I have some fresh warm water? And a warm piece of flannel would be helpful.'

Biesma gave the orders, and a servant rushed to fulfil Lippert's request. Meanwhile he rolled Frau Erler over again and began washing her face.

'She appears to have died in some distress,' he remarked. 'I fear that she knew what fate awaited her. The man, however, did not.'

'How can you tell?' I asked.

'The expression on their faces. But also, I beg you to look at their hands. The man's are undamaged; he did not use them to defend himself, presumably because he saw no threat. The woman's are cut in three places as she tried to fend off her assailant. If she had cut her own hand in a kitchen accident it is unlikely that she would harm both, and I cannot think of any way that she would slice the outer edge of her right palm.'

'That implies that the husband was killed before the wife.'

'I would think so. He does not appear to have tried to intervene to protect her, which any husband would surely do if he could.'

The servant arrived with the warm water and a towel. Lippert used his finger to pull loose earth from Frau Erler's mouth, then poured some warm water in and allowed it to drain out, all the while holding the warm towel against the junction of her jaw with her cheek. When this operation was complete he laid her gently on her back and I could see that he had been able to push her face into a more composed attitude. He closed her eyes and rested her head on the folded towel.

'I think if someone were to brush her hair she would have a much better appearance for her burial,' he said quietly.

Next he used a brush to flick the earth from their garments. 'I'm afraid the floor will need sweeping when I'm done,' he said with a smile. He carefully drew round Frau Erler's hands and marked the wounds on his drawing, before noting the stab wounds on their clothes. 'Now, if you gentlemen will assist me, we will remove their clothes to examine their injuries better. Let us start with the man.'

Each item of clothing was carefully removed and held up to the light to examine it for cuts or tears. Herr Erler's undershirt was quite ancient, but Lippert claimed he could distinguish between cuts and old tears.

'So,' Lippert summarised, 'we have a wound to the back which has obviously bled copiously. I suspect we will find that the knife penetrated one of the great blood vessels. The victim would quickly feel faint from loss of blood and would no doubt collapse. This second wound to the chest has missed the heart but from its angle I imagine it will have pierced the right lung. We will verify these suppositions when I open the body. There are then two further cuts to the abdomen but the absence of blood in the wound might suggest that the man was already dead when they happened. It is, of course, hard to be sure given the time that has elapsed since their death and the fact that they have been underground. Would you prefer me to open the man now, or examine the woman first?'

'The woman, I think, if you please,' I said. I hoped that some sort of urgent business would call me away before any dissection occurred, and had half a mind to send Biesma downstairs to see if he could find some.

Lippert repeated his earlier actions. I regretted the need to undress a woman and averted my gaze so far as possible, until Lippert insisted that I should look at something interesting. 'My, my! This is very strange.' He was holding her skirt up to the light.

'It's an ordinary woollen skirt,' I remarked. 'I don't see anything of interest here.'

'It's what you don't see that intrigues me,' Lippert answered. 'There are no cuts in the cloth, and yet the woman has stab marks in her thighs.'

'Which means?'

Lippert frowned as he folded the skirt carefully. 'Which means that her attacker lifted her skirts to stab her beneath. And since these wounds are similarly bloodless, he seems to have done it after her death.'

I now comprehended his confusion. Why would her son have done that?

CHAPTER FIFTEEN

I was understandably relieved when a messenger came to tell me that the two young women were making a fuss about still being imprisoned. This allowed me to retire from Lippert's examination of the corpses while he was still making the large central incision so I invited him to use my office to write his report when he had finished if he so wished.

The guards had locked Griselda and Brida in a small chamber leading onto a winding staircase because it had a stout lockable door and no windows that would open. Unfortunately, it was also rather small, so the two of them had been quite uncomfortable, and they were in a particularly ungracious mood when I visited them, of the kind that young women of that age specialise in.

'We haven't done anything wrong,' Brida protested.

'Apart from running away from home,' I countered.

'That's not illegal,' Griselda argued.

'No, but it caused distress to your parents.'

'Not to our mother. She's dead.'

'I'm sorry to hear that, but what about your father?'

'He doesn't care about us.'

'If he cared about us he wouldn't be trying to marry us off to the highest bidder,' Brida grumbled.

'Perhaps it is because he cares about you that he is trying to secure your future,' I suggested. 'He is seeking to ensure that your future husband is able to keep you free from want.'

'But I don't love the wine merchant's son!' Griselda snapped, as if that had anything to do with marriage.

'Have you told your father this?' I asked.

'Dozens of times! But he just keeps saying that Hans has no prospects and I'll starve if I marry him.'

'Who is Hans?'

Griselda rolled her eyes as if I was a passing village idiot she had to entertain. 'My beau. He's a charcoal burner.'

'And therefore lives a hand-to-mouth existence. I've never known a rich charcoal burner.' Actually I doubt I've ever known a charcoal burner of any kind, but let that pass.

'I don't mind being poor if I can be with him. We'll have each other.'

I could see from the dopey look in Brida's eyes that she was infected with the same sickness. 'And have you got a boyfriend too?' I asked her.

'No, I'm too young. But that doesn't stop Papa trying to introduce me to Maximilian the chandler. I mean, he's ancient! He must be at least thirty.'

One of the advantages of being a Governor is that you can just make up laws on the spot and nobody can challenge you, because if they are not laws now, they will be once you write them down and seal them, so I felt justified in creating one at this point. 'You don't seem to realise that if you leave home without your father's consent you can be brought to the castle and branded on the forehead with the letter R for runaway. And who will look at a girl with such a mark of shame on her?'

As I anticipated, this had a sobering effect on them. Young women of that age inspect their skin in looking glasses for signs of any blemish, so the prospect of being scarred in this way was truly horrible for them.

'It is a measure of your father's love for you that he has not demanded such punishment,' I continued.

'Only because he couldn't get a good price for us if he did,' Brida mumbled.

I felt that some soothing concession might be necessary. 'I will speak to your father and ensure that he knows the strength of your feelings. But he is your father and I cannot overrule him in this matter.'

The sisters seemed to understand this, even if they still felt themselves aggrieved. There was no time like the present, I thought, and decided that I would call on their father without an appointment so as to give him the glad news that his daughters had been recovered unharmed, and to attempt to influence his thoughts about their future.

I might as well have saved my breath. The fool kept talking about his rights, and his needs, and his future, and gave little heed to his daughters' feelings.

'I cannot keep them all my days. God's blood, but they're expensive enough now! They cost me a fortune in perfumes and clothes. Oh, they may say that these things don't matter and that they'd be happy enough with that charcoal burner or someone like him so long as he loved them, but wait until the first time he tells them they can't have something because he doesn't have the money. They'll sing a different tune then, by Heaven!'

'No doubt there is much truth in what you say,' I replied, seeking to placate him, 'but the world looks very different when one is young.'

'Not different enough if you ask me. I'll take them back, but I'll have their rooms stripped of everything I've ever given them and they can have a taste of their futures. After a week or so I think they'll see it my way.'

I was at a considerable disadvantage in this conversation, not being the father of daughters (or, indeed, sons) so I hesitated to offer any guidance, but I foresaw a repetition of this lamentable episode if he persisted in his belligerence.

'May I offer some advice?' I said. 'They are your daughters, of course, and you are entitled to treat them as you wish, but perhaps they would be more pliable if no mention were made of marriage for a little while.'

'And suppose Wolfgang marries someone else in the meantime, where will we be then?'

'Wolfgang?'

'The wine merchant's son.'

'Is that likely?'

'You never know. It could happen at any time.'

'How old is he?'

'Forty-one.'

'If he has lived forty-one years without marrying it is surely unlikely that he will precipitately do so now,' I ventured.

'He can't be too choosy at his age. And opportunities like my Griselda don't come around that often these days.'

'Have you spoken to him to determine his feelings?'

'Certainly not. It would be most improper. I have conducted the negotiations through his father.'

'But you believe that he is keen to marry your daughter? He is, after all, of age and well able to make his own decisions.'

'And so is she!'

'But you won't allow her to do so.'

'I meant that she is of age. Only a fool lets a woman make her own decisions.'

At that moment I dearly missed my grandmother. If she had heard that I might well have had another murder on my hands and been compelled to recuse myself from the trial. She could throw a clog better than anyone I have ever known, as the lumps on my grandfather's head could testify. I could not hope to match her invective, so I did not try.

'Perhaps,' I said, 'but only a fool would disregard his daughter's happiness just to prove himself right. Remember what the Bible tells us in Paul's Epistle to the Ephesians, chapter six: "Fathers, do not provoke your children to anger, but bring them up in the discipline and instruction of the Lord." We are called to love our children.'

'Aye, and Proverbs, chapter twenty-two tells us "Start children off on the way they should go, and even when they are old they will not turn from it." That's what I'm doing, Governor.'

I gave up at this point, and resolved to keep the sisters locked up until the family saw sense. Maybe they would consider entering a convent, I thought.

And it was at that moment that my brain returned to an answer I had considered for one of my problems. I should have acted on it before, but my brain was overtaxed with so many duties pressed upon it that it was not functioning to its usual high level of efficiency, a fact amply demonstrated when I left the house and absentmindedly stepped in a pile of horse dung just outside the door, and was compelled to endure the journey back to the castle with one foot dangling in mid-air so as not to soil the interior of the carriage. I know there would be someone to clean it, but why should I give servants any more work than was necessary?

I arrived back at the castle, read Lippert's report carefully, and called for a beaker of beer on the grounds that if I was going to drink anything beer was better for me than a flask of wine, of which I was drinking too much. I began to understand why princes and governors eat and drink so freely. It's boring administering places, and the decisions you have to make oppress you. However, so absorbed was I in Lippert's report that I neglectfully called for a second beaker before I had drunk the first, and then felt compelled to drink them both rather than be the cause of waste, which I abhor. That is why I doggedly eat Albrecht's food when men of lesser moral character throw it to the dogs in the street; that, and the fact that I quite like dogs and see no reason to torment them in such a way.

Lippert's report was as comprehensive as one could hope given the time that the bodies had been in the earth. His conclusions were that the husband had been killed by a stab wound in the back that penetrated his right kidney. He had then been stabbed again in the neck as he fell, because the angle of the wound showed that he had been pierced vertically from above and it was hard to conceive of any man being tall enough to do that if the victim had been standing. There were other wounds made post-mortem, in Lippert's opinion, but those two had been sufficient to kill him. He would have bled quite profusely, particularly from the neck wound, and may well have died very quickly thereafter.

The man did not appear to have defended himself at all, so had presumably been taken by surprise; not so the woman, who had some skin and blood under her fingernails as if she had clawed at her assailant. There was not much, but then, as Lippert pointed out, the space under the fingernails will not admit of much. If only enquiries had been put in hand sooner it might have been possible to examine Hubert Erler for scratches and either condemn or exonerate him accordingly, but he had been so roughly used in prison that the poor man was covered in cuts and scratches.

Having delivered himself of all the facts that he could, Lippert added a conjecture, carefully labelled as such. He wondered whether it was frustration with the woman's self-defence that had caused her killer to make the post-mortem stab wounds in her thighs. It was, Lippert noted, a clear demonstration of spite or anger, particularly since it did not appear that he had any carnal intent upon her. Lippert confessed that it would have been hard to detect interference of that sort after her interment, but there was no ill-usage of her private areas suggestive of an assault there, for which I offered a silent prayer of thanks.

However, one aspect of Lippert's report did give me something to grab hold of. He thought it very unlikely that the assailant could have inflicted the neck wound on the husband without being heavily spattered with blood. Now, I had not had the chance to examine them closely, but I was confident that Hubert Erler's garments were not much bloodied. There had been some on his boots, perhaps, and a little on his shirt, but not much. Could he possibly have changed his clothes before burying his parents, in which event the soiled ones should still be in the cottage, because nobody had referred to a bonfire or other means of disposal? Did he even possess another suit of clothes?

Tap came in to tell me that the kitchen was enquiring whether I intended to dine in the hall or would prefer a trencher brought to my desk.

'Hm? Oh, I don't have much of an appetite, Tap. Just some bread and cheese will suffice.'

'Very good, Governor.'

'Tap, before you go, are you really a manservant?'

'Excellency?'

'You're not one of Pringle's soldiers in disguise, or a master archer or trained assassin, by any chance?'

'No, Excellency. I am a manservant.'

'Good. Then perhaps you can enlighten me. How easy is it to remove blood from a leather jerkin?'

'Once it's set, fiendishly difficult, Governor, unless you don't mind what the leather looks like. You can sometimes use soap if you're quick after the staining, but it may change the colour of the leather, and you can't scrub hard or you'll spoil the surface. But then if the leather is stained anyway you may have nothing to lose by making the attempt. Why, Governor, have you bled on yours?'

'I don't have a jerkin, Tap.'

The man would have known that if he had paid the least attention to my dress. Despite his claims to the contrary, I was inclined to suppose that he was really an agent of Pringle's with some ulterior motive or primary task. Whatever it was, attending to my comfort did not seem to be a major part of his work.

'No, Governor.'

'I was wondering about someone else's jerkin.'

'Whose would that be then, Governor?'

'It doesn't matter, Tap.'

'Very good, Governor.'

The imbecile stood in front of me awaiting instructions.

'I thought you were going to fetch me some bread and cheese, Tap.'

'I am, Governor, as soon as you dismiss me.'

'What? Oh, very good, Tap. Dismiss.'

He grinned happily and went about his business, leaving me to reflect that he was undoubtedly a military man. That sort of obstinate refusal to make any decisions oneself without an instruction is only found in the army. It baffles me that we ever win any wars, given the stupidity of our soldiers. I can only assume that the other side must be worse.

I was still turning this over in my mind when the door was flung open once more and Pringle strode in. He looked flustered, red of face and short of breath, as if some urgency had caused him to run instead of sending someone else. Despite this, he came to a halt before me and removed his hat with a deep bow. I could not fault him on grounds of elegance or courtesy.

'Good evening, Captain Pringle. Is something wrong?'

'Aye! Very wrong!' he replied, but then paused as if unsure how much to tell me.

'Would it make you feel better to share your troubles?' I asked solicitously.

'No,' he replied, 'but I'll do it anyway.' Having said that, he revealed no more for some moments, as if trying to suppress some great emotion. 'I have received a communication from the Stadhouder,' he said at length.

'Excellent!' I said. 'When will he get here?'

'He won't,' Pringle replied. 'He is not coming. And nor is his army.'

I don't know what that lumpy bit in your throat is called, but mine seemed to swell to twice its usual size and prevent anything other than an enormous gulp. 'Not coming?' I whispered.

'It seems not. I regret, Governor, that we have both been deceived. No doubt for the very best reasons,' he added hurriedly, just in case anyone connected to William was spying on us.

We stood in silence, Pringle because he had no more to say, and I, because I had lost the power of speech.

'Not coming now, or not coming at all?' I croaked.

'Not at all.'

I could not have been more surprised if I had been told that the Virgin Mary was a man. 'The Stadhouder isn't coming?'

'That's what I said.'

'But why?'

It is telling that amidst all the turbulent messages circling within my head, this was the first to escape. Had I upset him somehow?

'It has all been a ruse.'

'A ruse?' I shrieked, before remembering that this was confidential information and therefore repeated the question in an urgent whisper. 'A ruse?'

Pringle nodded. 'I am ordered to take my men and march them at full speed to the coast where they will be embarking on ships to invade England.'

'England? Not France?'

'I'm afraid not. William has been invited by sundry leading men of that country to land there and claim the throne for his wife. King James is to be cast out.'

I lowered my voice once more. 'Is this a real invitation or one of those documents conveniently found in a monastery somewhere if you pay the monks enough?' I asked.

'It seems to be real. I understand your old friend Compton is one of the signatories.'

I had known Henry Compton, Bishop of London, above twelve years and had great respect for him. We got along well and he had a library of over two thousand volumes. A man who collects books so diligently must have much to commend him.

'So why were we sent here?'

'To put the English off their guard. If their agents heard of an army being gathered they might have stiffened their defences, but when they saw so many men bound for France they must have relaxed.'

'Let me put this another way. Why me?'

This seemed to spark a recollection in Pringle, who reached inside his doublet to retrieve a small letter which he held towards me. 'This was inside my letter. It is addressed to you. You may recognise the handwriting.'

Who wouldn't? William had an abominable hand. Even in strong light it was difficult to read. By a dim candle in the late evening it was well-nigh impossible. I sent for more candles and wine and when they were brought I settled down to hear whatever inadequate excuse the Stadhouder had for such shoddy treatment of a faithful servant.

[Yes, Van der Meer, I mean me.]

CHAPTER SIXTEEN

'This is a difficult letter to write,' William began. *If it is difficult for you to write*, I thought, *imagine what it feels like to have to read it.* 'I have taken advantage of your good nature, which would be unpardonable were it not in the national interest,' he continued. *How can it be in the national interest to trick a poor, inoffensive university lecturer?* I wondered.

[Van der Meer, if you are going to snigger all the time dictating this is going to take an age. Yes, you definitely sniggered. No, I don't believe it is catarrh.]

'I have been in secret correspondence with some of the leading men of England,' William wrote. 'This has required the help of a number of emissaries and, of course, I have been compelled to keep it from our loyal ambassador in London, Aernout van Citters.'

I had met Van Citters on a visit to London that I should much rather forget. He had treated me with great civility and for a moment I forgot the injustice done to me to empathise with him, before righteous rage overtook me once more.

'I regret that it has been necessary to mislead you slightly too.'

Slightly? I had been dragged away from my comfortable position in Leiden, my books and the pleasures of Steen's Inn under false pretence. I had been made to endure a life of luxury, the use of a carriage, this wretched gold chain over my shoulders, the damage done to my reputation by peremptorily confiscating the property of an entire county, and for what?

[I will not sit down and be tranquil, Van der Meer. If you think this is a passion you should have seen me at the time. Thirty years later I have calmed down considerably.]

'It was important to conceal my true intentions from King James,' William explained. 'I had not previously intended to take any action, but I am indebted to my sister-in-law Anne who has uncovered a frightful imposture. The Queen claims to have been delivered of a baby boy, the new heir to the throne of Great Britain, although everyone at court knows that it was smuggled into the palace inside a warming-pan and is no more her true son than I am. This shocking impersonation threatened to deprive my dear wife of her rights which, as a dutiful husband, I am bound to defend, hazarding my life if necessary.'

I suppose William could justifiably claim to be a dutiful husband. He was certainly fond of Princess Mary and had hardly any mistresses at all. Whether this was due to fidelity or a realisation that kept women are expensive, I would not care to say. It was also true that he was personally brave, if not positively reckless on the field of battle.

'Pringle,' I said, 'would you describe the Stadhouder as a brave soldier?'

The Scot gave the matter some short consideration. 'Well, he fights like a lunatic with St Vitus' dance, so I suppose he must be,' he answered.

'The likelihood of a second Catholic King has frightened the men I mentioned,' William continued, 'who were disposed to allow the King his foibles so long as they were not continued, and regarded the accession of the Princess Mary in due course as a guarantee that Great Britain would remain Protestant, but now they saw this fair prospect removed from their horizon. Having previously corresponded with me to ensure an orderly transition of power when the time was right, they now implored me to take action to prevent this masquerade leading their country to inevitable destruction.'

I need hardly add that I did not see the prospect of a Catholic King in quite that light, but then my opinion counts for very little in The Hague and nothing at all in London.

'I have reluctantly acquiesced in this proposal, and am about to invade to vindicate my wife's rights. I am anxious to avoid bloodshed, and will therefore offer to parley with the King on the basis that he may continue his reign untroubled so long as he publicly assents to Mary succeeding him on his death. If he will not agree, then I hope that a show of force on my part, and the evidence of abundant support for Mary on the part of England's leading men, will induce him to abdicate without the disagreeable necessity to wage war.'

I am not absolutely sure that William really regarded war as disagreeable, and I had little doubt that if James hesitated for one moment after receiving William's ultimatum then William would unsheathe his sword without reluctance or delay. Of course, all this was of secondary importance to the question of how I was going to be released from this irksome role now that the army were not coming. I had been banking on their commander making some arrangement to replace me with a military governor, and now it sounded as if the entire army was bound for England.

'Pringle, when do you leave?'

'Within the hour, Governor. I'll leave you a personal bodyguard — that troop of twenty or so.'

'Within the hour? That hardly gives you time to load up all the supplies you've gathered.'

'Indeed, Governor. That's why we're not taking them.'

'What am I meant to do with rations for twenty thousand men?'

'Are you feeling hungry?' Pringle asked, which I thought was not the most helpful thing he could have said.

'I'm being serious.'

Pringle stroked his chin thoughtfully. 'Well, each of my men will be told to take as much as he can conveniently carry, but given that their weapons are heavy that may not be a great deal. Whatever is left you can give as alms.'

'Could we return them to their owners?'

'No, for two reasons. First, we are their owners. Or at least William is. They're paid for, or will be once the money is shared out. Second, we have no idea where we got any particular item.'

I sighed. I seemed to be doing a lot of sighing. I found myself recalling the words of Lamentations Chapter One: Verse Twelve *Is it nothing to you, all ye that pass by? Behold, and see if there be any sorrow like unto my sorrow.* Not that I was feeling sorry for myself, you understand. 'Speaking of money, aren't you going to use that to pay your men?' I enquired.

'Good heavens, no. Disastrous thing to do. We never pay them in full. I might give them a small amount just to keep them keen. You can use the rest towards the compensation payments.'

This was all highly unsatisfactory, and the rest of William's letter brought me no comfort either.

'You may wonder why I invited you to undertake this task,' he wrote. 'The answer is simple. It was vital to the success of the deception that the major character should utterly believe that the feint was real. To make that possible, he had to be a man of unimpeachable honesty, so of course you came to mind. A lesser man might have betrayed the devious nature of the trick, but you are known to be incapable of dishonesty. If you believed in the plan then others would, and I am pleased to say that it has worked! We have received intelligence that Louis is moving soldiers to the north-east of France in anticipation of an attack. If we delay now he might concentrate sufficient men to threaten us. Now he will not dare do so because his troops might be needed in England. They will not get there, of course. I will fill the sea with warships to deter their crossing, but they do not know that yet.'

An awful fear came upon me that despite William's optimism the French would simply pour into Moers the moment he was known to have sailed for England. What would I do then? I resolved to ensure that all those near to me knew the French for "I surrender" in case it came in useful. Perhaps I should send Pringle's escort away to save themselves? They could achieve nothing in the face of a French army except sacrifice themselves to no good purpose. If the French meant to slaughter us they would do so whether we were defended or not.

I became aware that Pringle was shifting awkwardly from foot to foot.

'If there is nothing else, Governor, I have a busy hour ahead of me.'

'Yes, I understand.' I embraced him. 'God go with you and keep you safe.'

'Amen to that, Governor. And may He guard you too.'

Pringle strode to the door, turned and bowed flamboyantly one last time. 'If I may say so, I understand the Stadhouder's idea. He pays you quite a compliment but he is right. It is your transparent honesty that made the deception work, and it is the same honesty that will see you through the next few weeks. Do not allow any blame to attach to you, I pray.'

A lump came to my throat again. I was moved by his words. 'Thank you. Do you have any other advice for me before you go?'

He replaced his hat and thought for just the twinkling of an eye. 'Aye. If it all goes wrong on you, hang Fleckstein. It'll be popular with the locals and he'll probably end up that way anyway.'

And he was gone, as was my appetite for the bread and cheese Tap brought in.

I have had better nights' sleep. For a start, I could hear the clopping of hooves and the rumble of carts as the army started its night march on the way to the west. They would be tired when they reached the ships but then they could sleep as they crossed the ocean, I guessed, if sleep is possible on a ship, which I very much doubt based on my previous experience.

I decided the most useful thing I could do was to go to the chapel and pray. I am quite good at praying, once I have settled, and I had a few obvious things to pray for, chief amongst them being avoiding a lynching once the locals knew that the army had gone.

I was on my knees reciting the *Magnificat* when Biesma found me. He had the courtesy to wait until my lips stopped moving before speaking.

'There you are, Governor! I understand there has been a change in our circumstances during the night.'

There was a day in 1654 when a gunpowder store blew up in Delft and demolished a third of the city. Biesma was the sort of man who would have described that as a "disturbance".

'I have been deceived and deserted, Biesma! Dumped upon in the most egregious way!'

'There is some consternation in the streets, Governor. People are asking what is going on. I think we should make some kind of statement.'

'What kind of statement would that be, Biesma? "Be of good cheer, citizens. The French army will be here shortly to cut all your throats." How will that go down?'

'Very badly, I imagine, Governor. So we will not say that. But there is an opportunity to shape the public reaction to events.'

I had no idea what the man was talking about.

'Governor, the mob know only that the soldiers have gone. They are glad of that. If they were to come to believe that you had sent the army away, they would have great affection for you.'

'But it's a lie.'

'Not necessarily. You wanted the army to stop raiding the people, didn't you?'

'Yes, but…'

'So you had the intention.'

'But not the power.'

'With respect, Governor, they do not know that. Who ordered the army to leave?'

'The Stadhouder, I suppose.'

'And what are you if not the Stadhouder's man, sworn to uphold his commands? So if the Stadhouder says the army must go, it is your clear duty to tell them to do so.'

'Yes, but…'

'So if I were to draft an order to that effect and nail it to the castle gate after you have signed it, that would be perfectly proper.'

'Proper, but pointless. They have all gone.'

'We cannot know that. There may be one or two stragglers who have not heard the order. It could be backdated, I suppose.'

'No! It must bear today's date.'

'Well, that is no problem.' Biesma smiled. 'Much of the army did not leave until after midnight, which smudges over things very satisfactorily.'

I caved in. God forgive me, I was past caring. I just wanted to go home. 'As you wish,' I said.

'Thank you, Governor. I will bring the order for signing as soon as it is engrossed.'

'Thank you, Biesma. You're not a Jesuit, by any chance?'

'No, Governor. Why?'

'It's the sort of argument they're good at. I just wondered.'

Biesma did not leave me, but stayed before me like an angel who had not delivered the entirety of his message.

'Was there something else?'

'Only that I wondered whether you had given any thought to the supplies that the army has not taken. They are quite substantial.'

I had tossed and turned all night thinking about this. We had snatched them from hungry families and now they would go to waste. 'We must give them to the poor, Biesma.'

'I am delighted that you feel that way, Governor. I have drafted a proclamation here. You will see that any widow can claim a free measure of grain and assorted other items, as can any mother of three or more children. When we see how much remains I can come up with something else.'

'How will you prevent the widows coming back again?'

'Would it matter if they did? But we could take their names.'

'We can do better than that!' Now that I could see something positive to do I felt more energised. 'Biesma, let them bring a certificate from their minister of religion vouching for their entitlement. The ministers won't break the rules.'

'Excellent, Governor!'

I suddenly saw that if I had to be Governor of this place at least I could be the kind of enlightened despot I had always thought the country needed.

During the morning I drafted several other orders. One required all children aged seven to ten, both boys and girls, to go to school one day a week at no expense to their family, the teachers being paid by the Governor. Any shopkeeper found giving short measure was to be required to give double the deficiency not only to that customer, but to all others served that day, if they so requested. Alehouses were not to serve men who were already intoxicated under threat of losing their licence to brew and any man found drunk in the street would be barred from all alehouses for a week. In short, Moers underwent such a programme of reform as I doubt any land in Christendom had seen before.

Once I had breakfasted I remembered Princess Mary's parting words: "Master, I pray that whatever befall you will not think ill of us. We do what we do for the good of our countries."

She had known! Of course she had. William would have discussed his plans with her because it was on her behalf that he was invading. He had great respect for her common sense, to the point where he left her in charge of the country while he was abroad and… She would be in charge now! William might have gone overseas, but Mary would be managing the country from The Hague. If I wrote to her she would take pity on me and arrange for someone to be sent to replace me, ideally one who had experience of government but, if necessary, a complete buffoon so long as I could get back to Leiden.

I soon had two scribes working full-time on letters which I had feverishly dictated. I requested early payment of William's promissory notes, painting a picture of the extreme suffering of the people of Moers who might turn to rebellion if no money was forthcoming. I wrote to the University at Leiden to ask for a couple of students to be sent to teach the young children. I was even feeling benevolent towards undergraduates and would have accepted a pair of them, so long as they could recite the alphabet and do their own breeches up. Admittedly such stipulations would narrow the field a bit, but there must be a few young men who would welcome the opportunity for service, especially if the Rector fixed them with that sharp eye of his when he asked them.

I had another letter to write, but first I needed an interview with Alida Krul.

She cowered in the corner of her cell. When I say "her cell", I mean the cell she occupied along with others. There were women there whose company must have been repellent to a decent woman like mevrouw Krul, steeped as they were in every kind of vice. I asked for her to be brought out and placed on a bench in a quiet corner, given food and something to drink.

'Mevrouw,' I began, 'what religion are you?'

'Why, a Catholic, Governor. Many of us are here. Not that there's anything wrong with being Reformed,' she added quickly, in case I was offended.

'Have you thought of entering a nunnery?' I asked.

'A nunnery, Governor? No. Of course, it would be pleasing to spend time in prayer and become more learned, and I am not afraid of hard work.'

'The chief attraction, it seems to me,' I said, 'is that your husband could not enter there, nor could he reasonably object to your going.'

She smiled. 'That would teach the bastard!' she chirped. 'Begging your pardon, Governor.'

'I cannot guarantee acceptance,' I told her, 'but I know a kindly abbess here in Germany who might be willing to receive you. I will write to her today.'

Alida Krul dropped to her knees and kissed my hand. 'Bless you, Governor!'

'Now, there's no need for that,' I said, feeling very embarrassed. I felt even more embarrassed when she asked if I expected to enjoy her body to show her gratitude. 'Thank you for the offer, but no,' I said.

'Bless you for saying no,' she said, and kissed my hand once more.

Before I left I gave the jailer a few coins and told him to make her more comfortable. He had her moved to the small room where the two young women had been kept. It was small, but free of vermin. She seemed ridiculously happy to be there.

CHAPTER SEVENTEEN

The difficulty with my plan was that the delivery of letters is always rather uncertain. In this case, more so than usual, because while it was true that I knew a kindly abbess, the Abbess Mathilde whom I had met during one of my adventures in Maastricht, I had only a vague idea of the whereabouts of her convent. Fortunately, I bumped into a local Catholic priest as I went out to see how the free distribution of grain was going, and in conversation with him it was clear that her reputation was such that just about every priest in Germany must have known where to find her. Moreover, the priest had a man taking an important document to the local bishop, and that bishop would no doubt relay it to his brother bishop nearest to her, so that there was a good chance that the letter would be delivered unopened, particularly since it did not contain any money (my words, not his — I know what these bishops are like).

I returned at once and penned a letter couched in respectful but friendly terms to the Abbess Mathilde. I hoped that she remembered me as well as I remembered her. She combined a natural grace and beauty with a superb intellect. Knowing that she had a secure grasp of Latin I wrote to her in that language asking her agreement to receive Alida Krul. I had no idea how I would get her there if Mathilde accepted her, but I would find a way. I would take her there myself if need be, if I could find anyone who knew where it was and I still had the use of the carriage.

Feeling buoyed up by finally having one problem heading towards resolution I rashly decided to pay a visit to Hubert

Erler to see if I could shake him into giving a straightforward account of himself, but in no time my good mood was punctured as he resolutely refused to talk about the events that led to him burying his parents in the yard behind their house.

'You will realise, Herr Erler, that such actions are not easy to explain away innocently,' I said.

'You must think what you will, Governor,' he replied. 'I can say no more.'

I began to experience something of what the inquisitors had felt when they questioned Martin Luther. A man who just stands there repeating "Here I stand — I can do no other" is very frustrating to question.

'Herr Erler, your life is in peril here. You know that. I have the power to order your execution, and whatever my own feelings on the matter, I must carry out my duty. I cannot delay that indefinitely.'

Actually, if I did, who was going to stop me? But it cannot be good government for a magistrate of any kind to dispense sentences according to his personal whim, or to refrain from doing so for no good reason other than his instinct that there was more to this story than appeared at first sight.

'I am ready to hang, Governor,' he muttered.

I decided to try another tack, on ground that I would find rather more familiar. 'Consider this, then. Whatever I decide, no blame will attach to me because you give me no reason to save you. But in the world to come, when you stand before God's judgement seat, will he greet you as an unconfessed murderer or as a liar who shielded the true killer? Either way, I cannot imagine your eternal life will be comfortable.'

Erler blenched. It was clear that my words had wounded him, but after a moment or two he recovered his composure and returned to ignoring me once more.

'Take off your jerkin,' I ordered.

He obediently did so. I held out my hand and he gave it to me, whereupon I carried it to the door. The light in dungeons is not at all good, and I could not see much.

'I'll return it in a few minutes,' I announced, and took it out to the courtyard where I could examine it more closely. It was old and quite battered, the leather scuffed in places, and some of the stitching had begun to fray. It was stained as well, but none of the larger stains looked to me like blood. There might have been a small smear on the lower edge. Speculation without evidence is never good, but I could imagine that if he dragged his father's body to the grave the neck wound might have been at that height; but all in all I was quite convinced that if Lippert was right about the sequence of events on that fatal afternoon, Hubert Erler was not the murderer. So why did he persistently refuse to clear his name?

A man needs a good reason to put his own neck in the noose. He must have tender feelings towards the real killer. Is it possible that his father had killed his mother and then destroyed himself? It could hardly be the other way round, because of the post-mortem injuries inflicted on Frau Erler's thighs. It would be the shame that Hubert felt that his father had done this that would cause him to keep silent — ah, but that won't work! Lippert had said that both bodies had post-mortem wounds, and that cannot be when two people are dead. If Herr Erler had killed his wife he might have stabbed her again after death, then turned the knife on himself (though stabbing yourself in the kidney would take a bit of doing, in my view) but he could not have stabbed himself again after he was dead.

That left only one other person that we knew Hubert might be fond of; his sister, Anna. Was he protecting her from punishment? If so, why?

Fleckstein was in a funny mood. Ever since I had started dispensing alms to the poor he had been seething with anger which he found difficult to conceal. I did not know why, and in the end I had decided to do the scientific thing and ask him.

'It is not the way things are done, Governor,' was his explanation.

'What would you have done?' I asked — quite reasonably, I thought.

'It is not for me to say. You are the Governor, and I obey your commands.'

'No, Fleckstein, you don't get off as easily as that. What would you have advised me to do, if I had asked?'

'But you did not ask.'

'Suppose I had.'

'But you did not, so the question is hypothetical. And I do not answer hypothetical questions.'

Biesma decided to weigh in. 'It has made the Governor very popular.'

'It is not the Governor's job to be popular!' Fleckstein responded. 'Governors do not expect to be popular, if they are doing their work correctly.'

'So you think I am not doing this right?' I asked.

'That is not what I said,' Fleckstein snapped.

'It sounded quite like it to me,' I replied. I was not angry with him. In fact, I had come to the conclusion that I did not care what he thought of me, and for once when I said that about someone it was true. It was only intellectual curiosity that impelled me to ask him.

'I would not dare to criticise,' he protested.

'Let us not call it criticism. Let us call it a desire for self-improvement on my part. Surely you would not refuse to help in such a meritorious endeavour?'

Fleckstein hesitated before responding. One could almost see him calculating whether an obdurate refusal to assist my self-improvement would cast him in a bad light. Finally he decided that it would. 'If we give food to the poor without charge they have no incentive to work. We will soon be assailed with vagrants and other indolent people choking our streets because they have heard that food is given freely here. They will come here from other states.'

'They might,' I conceded, 'but they would have to be very well-informed because we have only been issuing free grain for a short while and it is nearly all gone. They might have a long and fruitless journey. And surely people who have settled lives, a home and a family are not going to risk all that to come here?'

'They might,' insisted Fleckstein, 'once word gets around that in Moers food without work is acceptable.'

'Fleckstein, they'd have to find Moers first. I didn't know where it was when I was appointed Governor of the place! It's a tiny pimple on the backside of Germany. It's not a land of milk and honey.'

'To us it is!' Fleckstein retorted. 'It is our home, and we don't want it filled with foreign layabouts. Or home-grown layabouts, for that matter.'

'Well, there we are agreed,' I replied with spirit.

'Are we?' Fleckstein asked.

'Of course. I want to leave Moers in a prosperous state.'

'You're leaving?'

'Eventually. Who knows when?' *Who does, indeed?* I thought.

In all the commotion I had quite forgotten that I had asked the parents of the young man Donk to visit me. They appeared that afternoon, she in her best bonnet and he in a well-brushed — and well-worn — dark suit. I invited them to sit, which seemed to surprise them.

'Tell me about your son,' I began.

'Bruno was a good lad,' mevrouw Donk began. 'Big for his age all his life, and he grew stronger when he followed his dad into foresting.'

'He was a handy woodworker,' her husband interjected. 'But he hadn't the patience for intricate work.'

'You will know,' I said, 'that I have to decide what to do with Calvin Wisse.'

They nodded silently.

'What do you think I should do with him?' I continued.

'We?' the mother stammered.

'I'd like to hear your thoughts on this. You must miss your son, and I hear your hopes were pinned on him to look after you in your old age.'

'I can still work, God be praised,' the man said defiantly. 'I'm not ancient yet.'

'No, you're not. You see, the lawyers tell me I must have Wisse hanged. Is that what you think too?'

Mevrouw Donk clapped her hand over her mouth in shock. 'Hanged? What good will that do? Will it bring Bruno back?'

'No, but there is no punishment that can do that.'

'I could not do that to Elisabeth,' the woman continued.

'Elisabeth?'

'Calvin's mother.'

It had never dawned on me that the two families would be acquainted with each other. 'You know her?'

'Of course. We've often gone to market together. And Calvin was a sweet little boy. Not so little now, though.'

'Accidents happen,' her husband said. 'You can't hang a boy for an accident. He wouldn't have harmed Bruno on purpose.'

'So you're certain you don't want him hanged?'

The couple looked at each other. 'Certain,' they chorused.

I could hear the steam hissing from Fleckstein's ears behind me. The scratching of his pen became louder as he scraped across the parchment.

'Fleckstein,' I called, 'would you kindly have Wisse brought here?'

'Now, Governor?' He dropped his voice. 'Do you think that's wise?'

'A lot of the things I do aren't wise, Fleckstein, but it's what I want.'

Fleckstein bowed and flounced off to give the necessary orders.

A short while later the door opened and Wisse was pushed in. He ran straight to the Donks and dropped to his knees before them, apologising for what had happened and for his part in it.

'Wisse, please stand,' I said in my firmest voice.

Wisse did so.

'You are charged with causing the death of Bruno Donk by your actions,' I said. 'Are you guilty or not guilty?'

He lifted his chin and tried to say the word, but only a cracked whisper came forth. He tried again. 'Guilty, if it please Your Excellency.'

'Very well. The sentence of this court is that you give fifty days of work each year to mijnheer and mevrouw Donk as long as they live. You are to take no payment, and you are to work as diligently as their son would have done. And if you are found drunk you may be brought back to me for further consideration, and hanging is not out of the question. Do you understand?'

He shook his head. 'No. I mean, yes, I understand, Governor.'

'Very well. Can you read and write?'

'A little, Governor.'

'Good. Fleckstein here will record that sentence and you will mark on the document to show that you have understood it and accept your sentence. Do not let me down, Wisse.'

He stood bewildered in the middle of the floor, making the place look untidy. Despite my orders he was fairly insanitary and while I am not overly fastidious I like to be able to breathe in without choking on fumes, so I waved him away.

'You may go,' I said.

I heard the sound of a nib splitting behind me, and Fleckstein growled a filthy word as he blotted his page.

Anna Erler had been quartered with the kitchen maids for a day or two while we examined her house, but had chosen to return and get on with trying to run the farm, so that was where I travelled to speak to her. I thought she might be more forthcoming on her own ground, so to speak.

Needless to say, Fleckstein was against it. I had not confided my thoughts about the matter to anyone, but he took the view that a woman who was already highly-strung was now three parts mad with grief and could not be trusted to behave properly in front of me.

Mad? No, I think not. Grief-stricken, certainly. She walked around as if dragging her own cloud with her. I was shocked to see how much weight she had lost in such a short time. She was sweeping the floor when I arrived and I could see her blouse clinging to her ribs as her arm moved.

She dropped the broom in surprise as Biesma and I knocked on the open door. [No, Van der Meer, we didn't each knock. Biesma did the actual knocking. Governors don't do their own knocking, you know. They have people to do it for them.]

'Governor! I — sorry, please sit — I don't have any drink but milk…'

'Thank you, I have not come for refreshment,' I said. 'I want you to tell me a little more about what happened on the day your parents died.'

'I have told all, Governor.'

'I don't think you have. There are things here that I do not understand but I'm sure we can sort them out with a little extra explanation.'

She blinked as if she had no understanding of the matter.

'Let us go back to the morning. What did you do?'

'Why, my work as usual.'

'And you ate at midday here?'

'Yes.'

'Was Hubert with you?'

'No, he had gone out.'

'When, exactly?'

'When? I don't know. He did a few things, but then he was going to inspect a ram. I didn't see him go but he must have left before midday. It's a fair walk to the farm where the ram was, above an hour, I'd say.'

'So you don't know exactly when he went?'

'No.'

'And when did you expect him back?'

'I don't know. Maybe mid-afternoon. It depended on how long it took him to make his mind up about the ram and make arrangements if he was content with the deal to put him to our ewes.'

'And your parents didn't leave throughout?'

'No.'

'So what did you do next?'

'I wasn't needed for the afternoon, so I thought I would visit a friend in town.'

'Was she expecting you?'

'No. It was a spur of the moment thing. But I expected she'd be home. Girls usually are, aren't they?'

'But she wasn't?'

'No. I had a wasted journey.'

'Can you give me your friend's name?'

'Why? She wasn't in. She doesn't know anything.'

'She can confirm to me that she wasn't at home.'

For some reason my questions seemed to bring out some high emotion in Anna Erler. Her voice had an unpleasant edge as she gave me the details.

'Helga. Helga Flock. She lives in the cooper's house just inside the south gate.'

'Thank you. I'll speak to her. And when you returned, what then?'

'It was terrible. The soldiers were taking Hubert away and saying he'd killed my parents.'

'Did you see your parents?'

Anna shook her head vigorously. 'No, he'd already buried them.'

'I see.' It was time for the one question I wanted an answer to more than any other. 'And why do you think he killed them?'

She burst into tears. 'I don't know! He won't tell me. He won't even talk to me. How can I know, if he shuns me?'

I had not the heart to tell her that he was shunning her because he knew she had killed their parents. It was clear now that if this girl Helga Flock even existed she would have been at home and would deny that Anna Erler even called. All I had to do was to establish that and the third case would be solved.

I had no wish to see Anna Erler go to the flames — as a parent-killer she would be burned alive — but nor did I want to hang an innocent man.

All in all, with Calvin Wisse released, Alida Krul on her way, God willing, to a safe refuge in a convent, and Anna Erler close to being proved a murderess I thought it was not a bad piece of work on my part. I had no wish to remain a Governor for one minute longer than necessary, but at least I was doing the job properly. Nobody could say I didn't know what I was doing.

That shows what I know.

CHAPTER EIGHTEEN

During much of my adult life I have found that I do some of my best thinking while I am asleep. If that sounds paradoxical, allow me to elaborate. Quite often when faced with a particularly knotty problem which I have been unable to disentangle all day I go to bed and wake to find that the answer is now clear to me. There have also been occasions when I struggled to express something well in a book or sermon, and somehow wake with exactly the right words on my lips. I have no idea how this happens.

However, during the summer of 1688 this miracle went into reverse. I went to bed very content, feeling that my problems were reducing and I could see a clear path before me, only to find that when morning came my mind had concocted some serious barriers to that happy outcome that had not previously presented themselves.

I had dined better than for some time past, and perhaps it was due to the unaccustomed richness of a sauce or a bad turnip, but my dreams soon turned into nightmares. It began with my feeling that I wished that I knew that my letter had reached Princess Mary; from that, I found myself wondering how William's invasion plans were going; and then the awful thought struck me that if they had met with disaster William could be dead by now; from which came the terrible realisation that only he knew he had promised to recall me from this hellhole and that if anything happened to him I could be stuck here for the rest of my natural life.

The only glimmer of hope I could see was that if James had triumphed he might launch a retaliatory invasion of my homeland, install himself as King or Stadhouder, and replace me along with all the other dignitaries of William's government. Of course, if that happened I might be released from Moers but then hanged. I had mixed feelings about that.

I had met James before, and I cannot say that our relationship was such that I could expect any favours from him. I had been instrumental in uncovering some double dealing that had upset his brother, King Charles II, and I doubted that even James' limited intellect had managed to forget that. At least I now knew that the Bishop of London was on William's side, and he was a formidable man, as well as a careful one. If he had committed himself to the opposition to James it could only be because he anticipated some likelihood of success.

Thus comforted (slightly) I had a little more breakfast to replace the one that had come back up again while reviewing my dreams and made my way to my office.

I was lonely. This strikes me as an astonishing admission, because I have long felt myself to be self-contained, comfortable in — even desiring — solitude, and yet my inability to exchange a few words with Mechtild, or even Albrecht, the fact that I could not simply walk to an inn and have a beaker of beer whenever I wanted — not that German beer compares well with Dutch, in my opinion — and that I could not spend a few hours with my nose buried in a book were all weighing heavily on me. I had even found myself thinking that the undergraduates I taught were not such bad chaps really, and chuckling to myself at some of the asinine infelicities in their essays as I recalled them.

I digress to note that many of the leading men in my land were undergraduates at Leiden once, and no doubt their lecturers then thought that the idea that they might ever be entrusted with positions of any responsibility at all was frankly risible. Of course, three or more extra years in the higher schools will have developed their talents further, but it just served to make me think that my undergraduates could not be such deadweights as I imagined. Then I shook my head violently because it was clearly disordered if it thought in such a way, and resolved to leave the German wine alone for a while.

I had not heard from Abbess Mathilde either, but this surprised me less. My letter to Princess Mary had been carried by a man from the guard who had changes of horses available to him. It would probably arrive within two to three days, if all went well, and he had been instructed to wait in The Hague for a reply. The missive to Mathilde, by contrast, had been carried to a bishop, then to another bishop with no great urgency, no doubt, and if the bishop forwarded it at all, he would take his time about it. The best hope I had was that if Mathilde ever discovered I had written to her and people had been dilatory in forwarding it I would not want to be in their shoes when she demanded an explanation. I conceived that a discussion between an aggrieved abbess and a mere bishop would be like a contest between a hungry cat and a three-legged mouse.

Have you ever noticed that just when you think things cannot possibly get worse, fate has a way of proving you wrong? I was just thinking about going out to find the young woman Helga Flock that Anna Erler had mentioned when Biesma appeared in the doorway. I could tell by the grave expression on his face that I was not going to like what he had to say.

'Governor, Heribert Krul is here demanding to see you.'

'He can demand all he likes. Why should I see him?'

'He says that if you do not restore his wife to him at once he will complain to the Stadhouder.'

'Excellent! Maybe the Stadhouder will agree with him and replace me, then we'd both be happy.'

'What am I to tell him, Governor?'

I bowed to the inevitable. 'Tell him I can grant him five minutes but make him wait ten before you bring him in.'

That should show him who was in charge here.

Normally I worked at an ordinary desk and chair, but there was a larger chair somewhat like a throne at the end of the room. It stood on a small dais which meant that I was a head higher than anyone speaking to me and they were kept a little distance away by the step.

Heribert Krul marched in, all swagger and bluster, momentarily stopped as he realised that I was not at my desk, then strode up to me in high dudgeon.

'I want —' he began, but was checked by Fleckstein of all people.

'Hat!' he yelled.

Krul snatched his hat off angrily.

'Bow!' Fleckstein continued, which Krul did.

I warmed a little to Fleckstein then. I am not pompous or puffed up with my own importance, but the office I hold demands some respect even if I do not.

[Van der Meer was unable to take dictation for a moment. I thought he was suffering an apoplexy, but it seems something went down the wrong way and forced him to cough. He is only in his middle years but I may have to get one of the physicians here to look at him. These paroxysms of coughing and spluttering are becoming more frequent.]

Krul stood with his hat in his hand. He was not a small man, nor well-proportioned. As he addressed me I couldn't help feeling that I was being spoken to by a barrel with legs.

'I have been patient,' he claimed, 'but you have still not restored my wife to me. This is taking an unreasonable time and I demand to know the excuse for this delay.'

'There is no excuse,' I said, 'but there may be a reason.'

'Excuse, reason, it's the same thing,' he claimed.

This, of course, was playing to my strengths, because linguistic pedantry is what I do for a living. Suddenly I felt I had the whip hand in this discussion.

'Not at all,' I said. 'An excuse implies fault and is an attempt to mitigate any blame for that apparent fault by demonstrating a limitation of freedom of action, thereby lessening responsibility. Where there is no blame there can be no excuse. A reason, on the other hand, is a justification or explanation of one's behaviour grounded on facts or logic and intended to enable the recipient of the reason to understand why events have turned out as they have.'

Krul goggled. Given more time I might have come up with a more satisfactory explication, but I thought it wasn't bad for something extemporised. Since he still appeared confused I furnished an example for him.

'If, for example, you are expected at church but are unable to attend due to a fever, the fever is the reason and a note from your mother is the excuse.'

'I don't have a mother,' he argued.

'My sympathy,' I answered. 'But you had one at some time.'

'Perhaps my wife could write a note for me, if she were not illegally imprisoned here,' he commented acerbically.

'I ask myself what your wife would write in such a note and whether it would be creditable to you.'

'I do not have to answer to anyone for the way I run my household,' he growled.

'You have to answer to God, as do we all. In the fifth chapter of the Epistle to the Ephesians, do we not read "Husbands, love your wives, even as Christ also loved the church, and gave himself for it."'

'I do love her, in my own way. It is because I care for her that I chastise her.'

'Is that what you call it? Breaking her bones, beating her mercilessly and inflicting indignities on her?' I was strongly moved by this vicious man's lack of contrition.

'Now, you listen to me —' he began.

'No, you listen to me!' I shouted back. 'Your wife will not be returned unless and until I am satisfied that she will be safe. And you may as well know now that she is giving thought to taking the veil.'

It was gratifying to see his lower jaw pumping up and down with no sound issuing from his mouth, looking like a freshly landed carp. At last he managed to gasp, 'Take the veil?'

'So I believe.'

'This is your doing!' he yelled, pointing accusingly at me. 'You've poisoned her mind against me.'

'I have done nothing of the sort. Your inhuman treatment of her has done that. You've had your answer; now, go!'

He hesitated as if about to offer violence to me. Biesma stepped between us, and Fleckstein summoned the guards from the doorway.

'Herr Krul is leaving,' he told them. 'And he won't be coming back.'

Krul reluctantly turned and stomped out.

'Thank you both,' I said, heaving a sigh of relief.

'I cannot abide disrespect,' Fleckstein told me; then he went and spoiled it all. 'If I may so, Governor, you bring this kind of thing on yourself by your easy-going nature. Men took no such liberties with your predecessor.'

'Except the men who had bribed him,' I could not resist throwing in.

'That was regrettable,' Fleckstein conceded, 'but those concerned have been punished accordingly.'

Being sent to the East Indies was certainly punishment. A Dutchman could live very well there, I was told, if he did not quibble about enslaving his fellow man, but no amount of luxury could stave off the fevers that claimed so many lives.

I picked up my hat and went in search of Helga Flock, taking Fleckstein with me in case an interpreter was needed, and leaving Biesma to draw up a few important papers. I also charged him to find me at once if a letter arrived from Princess Mary.

'Do you know this woman Flock?' I asked Fleckstein, who seemed to be enjoying riding beside me in my official carriage.

'I do not,' Fleckstein answered. 'But everyone knows Flock the cooper. His work is of a high standard.'

I have no idea how Fleckstein came to be a judge of coopering. To my way of thinking if a barrel does not leak, it's a good barrel. I had no notion that there could be more to it than that.

'The iron rings are meticulously adjusted to be perfectly horizontal,' Fleckstein explained with evident approval. Thank goodness he never saw any of my grandfather's woodwork.

We arrived at the cooper's house by the south gate, the picture of a barrel hanging over the door being something of a giveaway. Flock looked up in alarm as we entered.

'Excellencies!' he said. 'What brings you here?'

He hurriedly brushed off a bench in case we wanted to sit down. This brushing included removing a large and rather mangy-looking cat who had been sunning himself before his peace was disturbed, so I chose not to sit.

'We are looking for your daughter,' Fleckstein explained.

'My daughter. Which one? I have four.'

I immediately felt some sympathy for a man who had to endure the chatter of four young girls. I have no idea how they do it, but some young women seem to be able to talk without the need to breathe.

'Helga,' Fleckstein added.

'If it please Your Excellency, she is at the well,' he replied. 'She will not be long.'

He invited us again to sit. Obviously Fleckstein would not do so unless I took a seat, so I sat down to spare him, though I took care to sit at the end of the bench that had been cat-free.

'While we wait, Herr Flock, you are welcome to continue with your work,' I said, 'though I wonder whether you know one of your daughter's friends.'

'Which one, Your Excellency?'

'Anna Erler.'

'Anna? The one whose parents were killed by her brother?'

'That remains to be proven,' I said tartly.

'I can't say I know her,' Flock replied. 'Say rather than I know *of* her.'

'And what do you know of her?'

'Men say she's a feisty little madam. Her poor parents have been trying to find a husband for her but her reputation goes before her. Who'd want to marry a grumpy little minx?'

Before I could get a word in he continued his discussion of a woman he had said he only knew slightly.

'Of course, the parents are to blame for not reining her in. This is what happens when you let girls get involved in important matters like this. You can't blame Anna for digging her heels in if she has never been corrected. A couple of blows of the strap and she'd soon see things her father's way. Spare the rod and spoil the child, they say.'

'You think her parents indulged her?'

'I'm only going on what my Helga has said, mind. Anna has these foolish notions about marrying for love. I thank the Almighty none of my girls are infected with such foolishness.'

His diatribe was interrupted by the arrival of a young woman with a large pitcher on her head who was introduced to us by her father.

'This is Helga. Helga, these gentlemen are the Governor and … someone else.'

'Herr Fleckstein is my secretary,' I explained.

'Herr Doctor Fleckstein,' he corrected me.

'Of course. My apologies. Helga, we are here to ask some questions about Anna Erler. We believe that you know her.'

'Yes, if it please Your Excellency,' she said, and bobbed in a curtsey.

'And you know, I believe, that her parents were recently found dead?'

'Yes, if it please Your Excellency,' she said, and bobbed in a curtsey.

'Helga, there is no need to curtsey every time you speak to me. Once is quite enough.' Actually I would not have minded if nobody ever did it, but this was not the time to get into that. 'Do you recall the day that they died?' I asked.

'Yes, if it please Your Excellency.'

'There's no need to add "if it please Your Excellency" all the time either, but thank you for your courtesy.'

'Thank you, Your Excellency.'

'Helga, Anna said she came to visit you that afternoon but you were not at home. Can you remember where you were?'

'Yes, Your Excellency.'

And then there was silence.

'It would help if you told us where you were,' I prompted.

'Oh, yes. I was at my mother's grave.'

'And you're sure of that?'

'Yes, Your Excellency. It was a Tuesday, you see, and my sisters and I go every Tuesday to tidy it and put a posy there. By rights, we should go on a Wednesday, because it was a Wednesday when Mother died, but that's a busy day for Father and he needs us here, so we always go on a Tuesday.'

'And is this widely known?' I asked.

'Begging your pardon, Your Excellency. How do you mean?'

'Do many people know you go there every Tuesday?'

'I couldn't say, Your Excellency. We make no secret of it.'

If Anna knew, then she could fabricate an alibi of sorts for herself. She could say she had come for Helga but found no answer at the door and it would be hard to prove otherwise. I began to think that Anna Erler was more cunning than I had supposed.

I was about to leave when Fleckstein interrupted. 'By your leave, Governor, may I ask a question?'

'Ask away, Fleckstein.'

'Helga, we have heard that Anna's parents had arranged a marriage for her with a man called Martin Laut. Had you heard of this?'

Helga cast her eyes downwards. 'Yes, sir. Anna was upset about it. She didn't want to marry him.'

'Why was that?'

'She said she wanted to make her own choice and marry one who loved her. Herr Laut has been looking for a wife for a while but she did not want to be his. She didn't think he loved her.'

'Then why did he want to marry her?' I interrupted. 'Surely she doesn't have a large dowry?'

'No, but Herr Laut is not expecting a large dowry. He has enough to live on and his own house. He wanted a wife to run his household and because everyone else has one, I suppose. It isn't good for a man to be on his own.'

I might have disputed that in other circumstances, but for now I did not argue. 'Where might we find this fellow Laut?' I asked.

'He works at the school, Your Excellency. He teaches there, though his great love is music and he gives music and dancing lessons in a room above. He lives in a house alongside.'

I thanked Helga and her father and motioned to Fleckstein to return to the carriage. I had noticed him out of the corner of my eye inspecting the finished barrels to check that the hoops were straight. I clearly was not giving him enough to occupy his mind.

'Well, Fleckstein,' I said when we were sitting in the carriage, 'what did you learn from that?'

'Helga is an observant young woman, and Anna Erler is a wicked one,' he replied.

At last we agreed about something.

CHAPTER NINETEEN

It never rains but it pours, they say.

When I got back to the castle I found Biesma looking very perturbed. A young man was kneeling on the floor in front of him looking rather dejected.

'Who is this?' I asked.

'His name is Jakob Gross,' came the reply. 'He is seventeen years old and he has been brought here by the constables.'

'Why?' I enquired, and saw him redden considerably.

'He was caught *in flagrante delicto* with a sow,' Biesma told me. He was blushing quite a bit himself.

'I'm sorry, for a moment there I thought you said a sow.'

'I did, Governor.'

'Is this true?' I asked Gross.

'Yes, if it please Your Excellency,' he whispered.

'I see,' I said, though actually I didn't. That is, I understood the charge and the confession, and I understand such things go on in country areas from time to time. I just couldn't understand what impels men to assault farm animals in this way.

Fleckstein was not troubled in the least by the question of motive.

'We have a confession, Governor, and the law is clear. Both he and the pig must hang.'

'Fleckstein, are there any crimes in Moers for which hanging is not the penalty?'

He ignored my question.

'I said, are there any —'

'I heard, Governor. I'm still thinking.'

'And?'

'Brewing beer without a permit is one. Then there's —'

'One will do, Fleckstein. Regardless of what this young man has done, why should the pig suffer?'

'To demonstrate that the proper order of things is being maintained.'

'Humans already know that. Is there any evidence that pigs are better informed as a result of one of their number being killed?'

'Man was given dominion over all creatures by God, Governor. It is both a power to be exercised and a duty to be met.'

'Correct me if I am wrong, but it seems to me that the pig did not consent to this activity. How can it be right to punish those who did not intend to sin?'

'The act is sinful, Governor. That is sufficient.'

'So, by your logic, Fleckstein, if this young man had raped a milkmaid they should both hang. Where has she done wrong in this?'

'She should have defended herself, to death if necessary, rather than submit.'

I looked around me but there was no heavy object on my desk with which to knock some sense into his skull.

'She should die rather than be violated? The rabbis of old taught that the preservation of life is the greatest good. If someone threatens to cut your throat unless you eat pork, eat the pork.'

'We are not bound by the teachings of Jews.'

'Our Lord himself was a Jew. Are we not bound by his teachings?'

'Does the Bible not teach us "There is neither Jew nor Greek: there is neither bond nor free: there is neither male nor female, for you are all one in Christ Jesus", Governor?'

'The Epistle to the Galatians. But that is not to say that Jesus stopped being a Jew, only that these things are not relevant within the Church.'

Poor Gross was squirming. It was bad enough being found doing what he had done without being subjected to a theological dispute about it.

'I feel magnanimous towards the sow, Fleckstein. I shall emulate Christ when he spoke to the woman taken in adultery, and tell the sow "Go, and now sin no more." John, chapter eight, verse eleven, I think.'

Gross attempted to stand and leave but Fleckstein forced him down again.

'The Governor was talking about the pig, not you.'

What was one to do with this young man? Frankly I had much more serious matters on my desk, though I supposed it to be part of my duties to ensure that the sows of Moers can go about their lives unmolested by randy youths.

'Whose sow is it?' I asked.

'My father's, if it please Your Excellency.'

'Does your father know about this?'

The boy was wild-eyed. 'No! Pray do not tell him.'

'You're going to have difficulty in keeping it from him when you're hanged in the town square and your crime is read to the crowd.'

Gross was sobbing by now.

'The townspeople will probably put a plaque on the square. I can see the inscription in my mind's eye: 1688: Near this spot Jakob the Pig-Molester was hanged. It will become an attraction for visitors to see. Your fame will spread far and wide.'

This may seem like cruel taunting, but I have some experience of disciplining young men. He cried so much I doubt he could pee for a week after.

'Now, Jakob, is that how you want to be remembered?'

'No, Your Excellency.'

'Will you do it again?'

'No, I swear. I'll never touch a pig as long as I live.'

'Or any other farm animal?'

'None of them.'

'Are you a Catholic, Jakob?'

'Yes, Your Excellency.'

'Then go straight to a priest and confess what you have done. Accept whatever penance he imposes, and then get back to work.'

'I can go?'

'But Governor, what if he abuses your charity and returns to his sin?' Fleckstein protested.

'If he does it again you can hang him twice,' I replied.

Gross rose to his feet and retreated to the door, clutching his cap and pausing in the doorway as if he half-expected me to say, "No, it's all a jest. Of course, you can't go, we're going to hang you." He hurriedly bowed, and then we heard his feet running along the corridor as fast as he was able. I made a mental note that if I was still here at the time of the Great Fair and it involved a foot-race it might be worth putting a few coppers on Jakob to win, if I were a betting man (and I'm not).

The temporary truce with Fleckstein seemed to be over. He was glowering at me, but sideways, in a furtive manner.

I quickly acquainted Biesma with the results of our interview with Helga Flock.

'It seems that Anna Erler knew that she could tell us that she had tried to visit Helga Flock because Helga would not be able to tell us she had not. Every Tuesday Helga takes flowers to her mother's grave, and this is widely known. Clearly Hubert Erler came home, found their parents dead and told Anna to clean herself up and burn any bloodstained clothes while he buried the bodies. Then he told her to make herself scarce in case anyone came so that she could claim she had been elsewhere at the time of the killings. I think we now know why Hubert Erler has refused to speak about the incident. If he does not hang then his sister does.'

'That is very chivalrous of him, Governor,' Biesma declared. 'And may I ask why she killed their parents?'

'She was being compelled to marry a man odious to her, Biesma. We should bring her here for formal questioning.'

'As you instruct, Governor.'

'You look doubtful, Biesma?'

'Not at all, Governor. No doubt any questions I might have will be answered during her interrogation.'

'Such as?'

'Well, I can understand why she would run away, but why come back? We brought her here during the search of the farm but she has had ample time to flee if she wished. If she walked to Duisburg she could vanish from our view quite easily. And we could not arrest her without leave of the authorities there.'

'There may be something in what you say, but…'

'Then this matter of the alibi confuses me. Surely she only needs an alibi if we know precisely when the crime was committed? If she planned this killing to take place when her brother was out — presumably because he would stop her — she would be alone in the farmhouse with her parents. Why concoct a story that proves you are elsewhere when her brother would know it could not be true?'

'But he clearly believes she is the killer, Biesma. Men do not put their own necks in the noose for complete strangers.'

Biesma fell quiet for a moment. I had outwitted him there.

'Then there is the matter of the arranged marriage,' he continued. 'A great many woman have marriages arranged for them, but very few murder their parents to escape one.'

'Very few, Biesma. Not none at all. And surely a brother and sister share such things. In whom would Anna confide her unhappiness if not in her brother. Perhaps the brother shares her view. Why else would he hide her crime for her?'

Biesma dropped the subject at this point, no doubt swayed by the strength of my argument, and went to make arrangements for Anna Erler to be brought to us. While we were waiting it occurred to me that I had not spent much time with God lately, so I took myself to the chapel to pray. A man's prayers are between him and God, but the reader may be sure that reference was made to my unhappiness, my unfitness for the task laid upon me, my desire to get home, my dislike of the man I was turning into, and my anger that I had been so cruelly deceived. God didn't say anything, so maybe He was feeling a bit sheepish about my situation.

When I returned there was no sign of Anna Erler. It appeared that she was not at the farm, so the soldiers were searching for her. I began to reproach myself for not realising her guilt earlier and thus imprisoning her before I had allowed her to escape.

However, Fleckstein had some good news for me. 'There is an official despatch awaiting you, Governor. Its bearer is refreshing himself but I can send for him so he can deliver it.'

'Please do,' I replied, trying hard not to sound excessively eager to see it.

A young army officer appeared wearing a hat with the largest orange cockade I had seen for some time. He saluted. 'Governor Mercurius?'

'Yes.'

'You will forgive me. I am charged with ensuring that I give this letter to Doctor Mercurius and to no other.'

'Of course. Well, you see I am wearing the chain of office.'

'You might have stolen it. The Princess said you could tell me the gift she gave you.'

'It was a copy of a book called *The Prince*.' I decided to say nothing about the ring. The fewer people who knew about that, the better.

'Thank you, Governor,' said the officer, stepping forward to hand me a letter.

'Thank you for bringing this to me. By all means return to your leisure but please do not leave without taking your farewell of me. I may have a reply.'

He saluted once more, turned smartly on his heel, and left us. Fleckstein and Biesma clearly had no intention of doing the same.

'Thank you, gentlemen. I need to be alone to read this.'

They left, somewhat reluctantly, and I sat at my desk and examined the letter carefully. I did not dare to open it in case it contained bad news, but on the other hand if it contained good news I did not want a second's delay. I carefully slit through Princess Mary's seal and opened the letter. A smaller letter fell out.

I opened the smaller one, which was handwritten by the Princess herself, a fact easily discerned by the poor spelling. She was a literate and intelligent woman, but her spelling was always eccentric. I have guarded that letter ever since, and can quote it exactly, but here I will correct the spelling for the convenience of the reader.

Dear Dr Mercurius,

I was saddened to hear of your difficulties. I have complete faith in your judgement and humanity and will support whatever decision you make on any matter. Please follow your conscience and treat my husband's people well.

The enterprise against my father is a mighty one and has been delayed by contrary winds, but I have just heard that they have finally set sail. There are above four hundred and fifty ships of all kinds, and a mighty army embarked thereon. The Stadhouder has set forth a declaration of his intent which I am told has been well received in England and so we have hopes of a good outcome, God willing.

Your own part in this has been considerable and I thank you for it. Our envoys the Heers van Zuylestein and van Dijkvelt had reported that King James did not believe that William would invade and leave his country unprotected against French attack. The deception that the army was headed for Moers was essential to put King Louis into a defensive rather than offensive stance. We hear that his troops erected barricades and traps to prevent your army's advance which will now have to be dismantled if they wish to move, but they show no sign of doing so. My husband had secured the co-operation of several princes of Germany whose armies are sufficient to hold the French back if need be.

This would not have been possible had you not been so convincing in the arrangements that you have made. I will ensure that as soon as the fate of my husband's expedition is clear I will make arrangements for your replacement. Only God knows when this will be, though I am advised that it is likely to be before Christmas for, if William has not met with success by then he will withdraw his troops rather than provision them for a long winter campaign.

If, as I hope, God favours our expedition William will send for me to go once more into England, so I may not be here when you return to your country. Who knows whether or when we shall meet again. Whatever befalls, I entertain only the fondest thoughts of you and of your attachment to our service and wish every kind of blessing upon you.

Mary

Christmas? I hoped she meant Christmas 1688 at the very latest, but even so that was around seven weeks away yet. Seven more weeks living in Satan's Back Passage? If it had been anyone other than Mary asking it of me I should have hired a horse and made my own way back to Leiden.

I glanced over the other letter. It was in formal language and conferred various additional powers on me. I was now, apparently, the Temporary Regent of Moers while the Prince of Orange (or Stadhouder, as I thought of him) was beyond the sea. I could now pardon anyone I liked, execute anyone I liked, or more to the point disliked, raise or lower taxes, grant various monopolies and licences and declare a fair or public holiday whenever I thought fit.

My first thought was to declare a public holiday and get blind drunk, staying that way until Christmas, but then I recollected that I had work to do, and I hated that feeling you have after a night of excessive drinking. I rarely over-imbibe, but sometimes in the university we have banquets and there are too many toasts to be drunk. The trouble with being drunk until Christmas was the prospect of being hungover until Twelfth Night.

I called Biesma and Fleckstein back in and told them to close the door. I showed them the formal letter granting me the additional powers but said nothing about the personal letter from Mary. 'It seems,' I told them, 'that I am here for the foreseeable future.'

'Shall I order church bells to be rung?' asked Biesma. He was in earnest about that, whereas if Fleckstein had said it I should have judged it to be sarcastic.

'I think that would be excessive,' I replied. 'But it makes the completion of the various cases before me all the more pressing. There is now no reason to delay. Please bring Franz Kirschbaum to me once more.'

Biesma bustled about his business.

'Are you not happy in my good fortune?' I asked Fleckstein.

'Congratulations, Governor,' Fleckstein replied, though his words were, in my view, lacking in due enthusiasm.

'Not Governor, but Regent,' I reminded him. 'However, since that will only serve to confuse the common people, let's keep that to ourselves for now, shall we?'

Kirschbaum came in.

'I have been considering your case,' I told him. 'You acknowledge that you wrote that William was not Count of Moers and that the sovereignty of this county should be transferred to another?'

'I do,' he said unrepentantly.

'You acknowledge that you did this in full knowledge of the law and its consequences for you if your authorship was detected?'

'I did.'

'William is not a man of tender feelings who would be hurt by mere words, neither does he wish to prevent men having liberty to say what they will, so long as the security of the realm is not threatened. I have no wish to take your hand off, Herr Kirschbaum. Let us see if we can avert that by coming to some kind of understanding.'

'What kind of understanding?' he asked.

Isn't it strange how people are often most suspicious when you are trying to do them a good turn? 'You could leave the country,' I suggested.

'This is my land. I have never known any other.'

'All the more reason to explore, then.'

'I would rather live here with one hand than go abroad with two.'

So that is the kind of idiot I am dealing with, I thought. There are things worth suffering for, and there are others that are not of much moment. William was a very benevolent ruler, but if you had never known any other, that might not be obvious to you. A few weeks in Berlin or Munich might have given him an alternative view of things.

'How do you live?' I asked him.

'What concern is it of yours?' he fired back.

'I need to be sure that you are not a vagrant. Do you have means of support?'

'I sell my pamphlets. I have a kitchen garden. I get by.'

'You see, William does not want to stop you writing pamphlets.' Kirschbaum relaxed. 'But I am about to make it illegal for anyone to buy them.'

Biesma looked shocked. Fleckstein grinned as if I had finally seen sense. Kirschbaum rose to anger.

'You can't do that!'

'I can,' I assured him. 'And what do you think that will do for your income? Three months in prison or a substantial fine is quite a deterrent to buying a pamphlet, I imagine.'

Kirschbaum looked crestfallen. 'You might as well cut my hand off and let me bleed to death,' he grumbled. I suppose I could forgive his gloomy tone given his prospects at that moment.

'I have an idea,' I said. 'It is high time that a history of the county was written. If you were to undertake this for me I could pay you twenty silver thalers now, and the same again when it is completed.'

It was not a huge sum for the work involved, but actually I was not much interested in the work, though no doubt I would read it; I read everything.

'The agreement, of course, is dependent on your not writing anything critical of the Government here while you are in my employ.'

I could see Kirschbaum wrestling with his conscience. He knew it was a transparent attempt to silence him, but forty thalers would give him a much more comfortable life, and he was still a young man. Perhaps he would find a taste for history.

'I can write what I like once the history is finished?'

'If finished to my satisfaction. And that of Dr Fleckstein, who will supervise your work.'

This came as a surprise to Fleckstein, who immediately preened himself. It was a surprise to me too. I hadn't thought of it before that moment and I had no idea what possessed me to say it.

'And I keep my hand?'

'You wouldn't be much use to me if you didn't have it, would you?'

Kirschbaum thought for a while in silence. 'All right. I'll do it.'

'Very good. You'll swear on a Bible to that effect and then you can go. Report to Dr Fleckstein in the morning. He will allocate a place for you to work.'

As he left I flopped back in my chair. Wisse had gone, Kirschbaum had gone, a plan was in place for Alida Krul. I just needed to find Anna Erler and then my work was done.

CHAPTER TWENTY

Someone famous in history — I forget exactly who — was often to be found mingling incognito with his subjects to see what they really thought. I needed some recreation and the company of the sort of people I had been accustomed to mix with before my elevation to the governorship. Admittedly they would be Germans, but that was a cross I was prepared to bear.

Thus I put away my papers, took off my chain of office, and what delight it was to be free of its weight, and sauntered down the hill into town in search of an inn. As I had expected, there were several.

There was some raucous singing in one, so I discounted that inn, just in case there was a resident lute-player, and pulled open the door of another called The Swan. As these places go, it was relatively salubrious. There was nobody unconscious on the floor and no sign of spilled blood. I found a stool and a potboy soon brought me a beaker of ale.

It so happened that I had taken a small book with me and I had just found my page when the man seated next to me started chatting.

'Haven't seen you here before,' he said. To my surprise he said it in Dutch (or something quite close to it), but then I noticed that my book was in Dutch.

'No, it's my first visit to Moers.'

'Well, it can't be pleasure so it must be business.'

'You could say that.'

'What trade are you in, then?'

'I work in an office,' I replied. I did not want to be specific if I could avoid it.

'Ah, yes. That explains your soft hands.'

'What do you do?'

'I buy lumber. The Germans have much more in the way of forest than us, you see, so it's not so expensive here. I get a bargeful shipped to Rotterdam now and again and I'm set up for months.'

'Isn't the shipping expensive?'

'Well, it would be, only the barges don't come empty, and I charge enough on what I bring here to cover the cost of the trip back too.'

He grinned, displaying a set of teeth. When I say "set" the reader is not to understand two orderly rows, but more a scattering of yellow pegs randomly situated in his mouth.

'I hear there's a new governor here,' I commented.

'That's right. Another Dutchman, like us. The locals don't like him but we know if he's Dutch he'll be all right, don't we?'

'What have the locals got against him?'

'They say he's William's lapdog.'

I could feel my hackles rising. Lapdog? Me? 'But I hear he's done some good things. He gave food to the poor, for example.'

'Yes,' my new friend conceded, 'but only after he took it off them first. He said he needed it for the army, but where's the army? Most of them never came here.'

'Maybe he expected the army, but their plans were changed.'

'He would say that, wouldn't he? Oh, I don't think a religious gent like him would pocket any of it. He's probably gets all he needs off the Church. But I bet his mates back in Amsterdam will do very nicely out of it.'

I felt quite indignant. I don't have any "mates" anywhere, but especially not in Amsterdam. I wouldn't lend most men there a bent stuiver, not that they need my money. Anyway, it was time to change the subject.

'What's the food like here?'

'Very German. No decent herring or crab.'

Given how far we were from the sea, this was hardly surprising. A herring swimming off the coast at Scheveningen back home could be on your plate an hour later, so of course it was fresh. A barmaid swayed past me carrying bowls of hot pottage that didn't smell too bad, so I asked for one of those. It seemed only polite to ask my fellow Dutchman to join me.

'Don't mind if I do,' he said cheerfully, and slurped from his spoon so loudly all conversation between us came to a halt.

The pottage smelled better than it tasted. I was just debating whether to finish my bowl or vomit now and get it over with when the door opened and two young men walked in. They laughed loudly as if one had just told a funny story, looked around them and spotted a bench in the corner that suited them. The taller one was dark-haired and wore forest green breeches and a small matching hat with a jaunty feather on one side. His coat was dark blue. The other man was shorter, blond-haired and was dressed in brown. They called for the boy to bring them wine and laughed their way to the shadows.

My companion scowled.

'Do you know them?' I enquired.

'No, and I've no wish to. There's something not quite right about them.'

'In what way?'

'I don't know. I just feel they're up to no good.'

The potboy was looking for beakers to fill so I signalled to him to come to us and asked him to refill both our beakers.

'Those gentlemen who just came in,' I said to the boy. 'Do you know who they are?'

'Aye, sir. The one in the blue and green is Herr Tolmund, who runs the playhouse. The older man is Herr Laut, the teacher.'

'Herr Laut? Martin Laut?'

'Aye, sir.'

I wanted a word with him. Perhaps he knew where Anna Erler was. I excused myself to the Dutchman, then realised I might need an interpreter and asked him to come with me. We crossed the inn to the corner and stood beside the men.

'Please forgive the interruption,' I said. 'I am Governor Mercurius.'

My speech was truncated by choking noises from the man beside me who was, no doubt, speedily reviewing our conversation to check whether he had said anything inappropriate about Governors.

'Your servant, sir,' said Tolmund, rising and giving an exaggeratedly courtly bow, as he might have done on the stage to ensure that it could be seen from fifty paces. Laut did not follow suit, but smirked a bit.

'I am anxious to speak to Jungfrau Erler, Herr Laut's fiancée, but she is not to be found. I wonder whether you are able to suggest where she might be.'

'I have not seen her,' Laut said. 'I think she may be embarrassed about seeing people, though of course she is in mourning. But I am anxious that our wedding should not be unduly delayed. Why are you looking for her?'

'I think she may be able to give me additional information,' I said guardedly. There was nothing to be gained by being too open, and Herr Laut might be distressed to hear that his wedding plans were to be disrupted by the arrest of his fiancée for murder. 'Does she have family nearby she might have gone to?'

'Her mother had a sister but I think she is dead too. There may be cousins, I suppose,' Laut told me.

'I'm a bachelor,' I said, 'so I'm curious to know what attracted you to Anna Erler.'

'I'll be frank,' he replied in a very offhand way. 'She is no great beauty, but I believe her to be a competent housekeeper and she has been well-schooled in obedience to her husband. What more can a man want?'

'She may bear you children,' said Tolmund, and laughed at the prospect.

'I expect she will,' Laut replied, adding, 'if God wills it.'

I thanked them for their help, apologising once more for interrupting their conversation, wished them a pleasant evening, and decided I had endured enough company for one evening, so I made my way back to the castle and, after a little contretemps with the dolt on the gate who did not recognise me without my chain on, I retired to my room to read a good book. A bit of Aquinas was just what I needed to relax after a hard day.

And so to bed.

CHAPTER TWENTY-ONE

The morning brought a very pleasant surprise in the form of a letter from Abbess Mathilde. It was, of course, in immaculate Latin, written, I think, in her own hand. She began by expressing her delight at hearing from me once again, assured me of her regular prayers for me — I made a note to tell her that I did the same for her — and then got straight to the point. Alida Krul would be very welcome, and she gave me directions for the journey. It could be walked in four or five days, but there were also stretches that might be negotiated by boat. Once past the city of Münster they were to ask for a place called Melle, and once there a man called Karl who was verger of a church there would show them the rest of the way. It all seemed very straightforward. I quickly scribbled an appreciative note of thanks and good wishes, sealed it, and went to make arrangements for the journey.

The party was ready to set off before midday. A young officer called Himst was deputed to escort my carriage, with five men to ride alongside. A carriage would be much less tiring for Frau Krul than walking the whole way, though it ruled out using a barge. I could manage without my carriage for a week, I thought. Anyway, if I needed one I could always buy one.

Another of the household staff, one of the laundry women, volunteered to go with Frau Krul as a chaperone and to help with any womanly needs. I had not seen her before, and when I clapped eyes on her I wondered if she really was a woman. She was certainly curvy in a number of places, though not necessarily symmetrically, but she had a square jaw and forearms that suggested that she would be useful in a brawl. Each woman carried a small bag, and I had given Himst a pouch of coins as a gift from me to the convent to thank them for taking Alida Krul.

I watched the procession plod slowly out of town. Once into open country no doubt they would pick up pace. Satisfied that the third of my cases was now concluded, I returned to my office to confer with Fleckstein and Biesma to devise a plan to find Anna Erler.

Biesma had a notion that it might be possible to find her with dogs. We would need some item of hers that bore a scent, but there are dogs that can follow a trail for miles across country. I had no better idea, so it was worth a try. Fleckstein knew a man who had a pair of hounds that might be suitable, so we asked him to come with us and together we walked out to the farm in search of some bedclothes that might carry her odour. It was at this point that I began to regret having lent Alida Krul my carriage. I am well accustomed to walking, of course. Like ninety-nine men and women out of a hundred, I walk everywhere in normal circumstances. I just had not walked much recently.

Needless to say, it started to rain. I was doubtful whether the dogs would still be able to detect the scent, but their owner thought that they might, so we plodded on, Biesma keeping our spirits up by singing psalms. I joined in, as did one of the dogs, probably more tunefully than me though with less adherence to the text.

We came to the Erlers' farm, and noted that the animals looked well cared for, though who was doing this we could not know. I went forward, pushed on the door and walked into the house, prepared to search it for something that the dogs could sniff. What I was not prepared for was to encounter Anna Erler. She grabbed a large knife and held it in front of her.

'What do you want?' she snarled, then, before I could answer, she added, 'Oh, it's you, Your Excellency,' and dropped the knife.

'Where have you been?' I asked.

'Here, Your Excellency. There is always work to do.'

'You were not here when the soldiers came for you a couple of days ago.'

'I was probably visiting Helga Flock,' she said. 'As you know, she was out when I last tried to see her.'

The impudence of the minx! Taunting us with her own transparent alibi!

It was at this point that I noticed that a dog which had been lying by the stove had got to its feet and was clearly unhappy that two other dogs were standing by its doorway. Not wanting to try to arrest Anna Erler while she had a knife to hand I moved towards her to move the knife out of her reach but the dog growled at me.

'I'm sorry,' she said, grabbing the dog by the scruff of its neck and pushing it back towards the stove. 'It was my father's dog and he doesn't understand where Pa has gone.'

'He looks like quite an old dog,' I remarked. The dog had watery eyes and some of the colour in its fur was fading so I felt on safe ground about that.

'We've had him about seven years. He was devoted to Pa.'

That led me to ponder why the dog had not attacked the attacker who killed his master, unless the dog knew them well. Without knowing it Anna Erler had just condemned herself out of her own mouth.

Her face crumpled and she began to weep. 'If only he had been here this might never have happened!' she wailed.

'Who?' I asked.

'Tumbler.'

'Is that the dog's name?'

She nodded. 'When he first came he used to roll and leap about like a tumbler at the fair.'

'And he wasn't here?'

'Pa insisted that if I was going into town I had to take the dog in case there were villains on the road.'

How very convenient that was for her story. 'Please gather whatever you need. I must take you to the castle for further questioning,' I said.

Anna Erler looked shocked. 'Why? I haven't done anything.'

'That will be for a court to decide. Please take the dog to someone who can care for it. We will wait while you do so but my colleague will go with you.'

I nodded at Biesma to conduct Anna to the Pittens' house. The murderess was not going to sneak off this time.

We were walking along the road into town when we were met by one of the castle guards with alarming news.

'Governor, our men at the north gate report that Heribert Krul and a group of men with cudgels have passed through the gate.'

I was grateful for the warning. It was unusual for people to show this level of initiative, and I can think of plenty of guards who would have taken the view that there was nothing remarkable about a bunch of men choosing to take their recreation together and carrying big sticks to do so. On the other hand, I was momentarily nonplussed. Even though I now knew this, what could I do about it, since Alida Krul had my carriage?

'Surely the carriage will outpace them?' I hissed to Biesma and Fleckstein.

'Not necessarily,' said Fleckstein. 'The carriage will have to stick to the track. Men on foot could cross the fields. They will still be at a disadvantage, but if Himst is sparing the horses they may be travelling no faster than a walk.'

'Where can we get a carriage?' I demanded.

To my surprise, Anna Erler had a suggestion. 'The man at the farm beyond the Pittens' has a cart. But it won't take us all.'

I can be very decisive when I want to be. Well, perhaps not very decisive — quite decisive would be a better way of describing it. Ordering Biesma to take Anna Erler to the castle, I asked Fleckstein to arrange to borrow the cart. The farmer, whose name was Obern, insisted on driving it himself, which was probably just as well, so Fleckstein and I jumped into the cart and we set off to intercept Heribert Krul.

Obern's horse was young and sprightly and kept up a steady trot. If only his cart had been better sprung. I was flung around in a most undignified manner and the only consolation was that Fleckstein seemed to be enjoying it even less than I was.

'Fleckstein, can you give Herr Obern directions?'

'I can, Governor, but it's fairly straightforward. Instead of going into the city we need to skirt its eastern edge, head eastwards and turn to the north. If fortune favours us we may meet them at the north end of the lake.'

This all meant nothing to me. Geography was never my strong point and I did not know the area at all, but if Fleckstein said there was a lake I was willing to take his word for it.

We rattled along the track at considerable risk to life and limb, and at a particular point Fleckstein ordered Obern to turn left and head along a path through the woods in a northerly direction. Progress was a little slower because there were tree roots to avoid and at intervals the light was poor because the trees were overhanging the path, but I began to feel hopeful that we might effect an interception before there were unseemly incidents. That feeling lasted nearly half a minute.

I cannot gauge distance well, but there was the unmistakable sound of a pistol being fired, and it was coming from somewhere not far in front of us. At my urging Obern drove the horse on, and soon we came out on the road that Himst should be following. We paused to listen, and could hear some clamour to our right. Thanks to Fleckstein's directions, we had managed to make up some of the distance and Obern drove his horse on again.

After a minute or two we heard a second gunshot, and soon we encountered a group of men running towards us carrying cudgels. I feared that they might intend us some mischief, but when they saw us they gave us a wide passage and kept running past us. It did not take much to discern that Heribert Krul was not one of them. For a start, he could barely run.

Within a very short time we discovered why. Krul was lying by the side of the track having been shot in the arm. It was a bad wound, and when we got closer we could see that the ball had clipped his upper arm and hit his chest. Himst had dismounted and was attempting to staunch the flow of blood with a kerchief.

'I had to shoot!' he exclaimed. 'I fired a warning shot but he kept trying to pull his wife from the carriage.'

'I understand,' I assured him. 'Let us get him to a surgeon. Can some of your men help me load him on the cart?'

When I said "help me" I really meant "follow my instructions" because that wretched chain precluded my doing much myself. Krul was quite a weight but eventually he was loaded on the cart. I walked over to the carriage to see how Frau Krul fared. She was pale, but resolute.

'He ought not to have done what he did, Governor,' she said, 'but I regret biting him.'

'You bit him?'

'And punched his hand as he gripped the carriage door.'

'But you are unharmed?'

'Yes, if it please Your Excellency.' She attempted to curtsey while sitting down, which looked rather odd.

'Driver, you had better move on, or you will be overtaken by the darkness. Himst, please continue.'

'One moment if I may, Governor,' said Fleckstein. 'Why did you not use your sword, Himst?'

Himst looked befuddled. 'If I drew the sword I would have to use it. I hoped that drawing the pistol would make him stop. When it did not I fired a warning shot over his head; and when that did not work I thought it would take too long to put the pistol away and draw the sword.'

'But you had to reload your gun,' Fleckstein persisted.

'I did,' admitted Himst, 'and it took some time. But I can only plead that in the heat of the moment one does strange things. I was hoping that a second warning shot would frighten them off but by the time I had reloaded, Krul was at the carriage and I feared that if he pulled his wife in front of him we would not be able to attack in case she was harmed. I did the only thing I could.'

'Fleckstein, let him go. The carriage needs to reach their inn before nightfall, and we have a suspect to question,' I said. 'And Herr Krul needs attention.'

He certainly did, but he never received it. Half an hour later he died in the cart.

CHAPTER TWENTY-TWO

I do not want any misunderstanding. I deeply regretted the death of Krul. I wish it had never happened; but he brought it on himself by attempting to interfere with the transportation of his wife to a place of safety. We delivered his body to his home for the servants to arrange his funeral, since it was clear that his wife would not do so. It turned out that his parents were still alive and they took charge of matters, though not without questioning me closely on the sequence of events. At times they were almost impertinent in their allegations, but one must make allowance for them given the loss of their son. It is my experience that however despicable a person is there is always someone to mourn him if you look hard enough.

Anyway, that discussion would not happen until the following day. For now, my chief concern was in getting Anna Erler to confess what she had done. I thought that this was unlikely but that I might be able to persuade her brother to admit just enough to hang her if I told him that I knew that he was not guilty, so he could drop this charade of shielding his wicked sister and let her face the consequences of her actions.

Hubert Erler got to his feet when Fleckstein and I entered the room where he was kept.

'You're a fool,' I told him. 'A chivalrous one, but still a fool. We have arrested your sister. I can prove that you did not commit this crime so you can give her up to her fate. Tell me what really happened.'

'You're mistaken,' he insisted.

'Really? You persist in this game? We know that you are keeping your silence because you know she is guilty.'

He made no answer but hung his head. It was as good as an admission.

'I'll tell you what happened,' I said. 'You went to look at the ram, exactly as you first said. You arrived back to find your parents dead and your sister gone, and you knew that she had killed them because they were persisting in attempting to marry her off to that fellow Laut. All you could do was to bury the bodies and perhaps tell anyone who asked that they had gone away somewhere. And it might have worked if Pitten hadn't turned up. At that point you knew that saying they were on a sudden journey would not work. If you were the murderer you might as well have killed Pitten too. You can only hang once however many you kill. The fact that you did not do so was an indicator of your innocence.'

Hubert sank to his knees and began to weep.

'The game is up,' I told him. 'Shortly I will question your sister, but I do not need a confession. We have enough evidence to prove her guilt regardless.'

Hubert choked back his tears and whispered something.

'I didn't hear that,' I told him.

'It is as you say,' he told us. 'Anna was determined not to marry Laut. She did not like him from the very start, but our parents were obstinate. They said it would secure her future and she would eventually come round. If only she had given me more time, I'm sure I could have won them round. They were wavering, I'm sure of it.'

'How do you mean?' I asked.

'The night before they died I waited until Anna went to bed, then I told them something that I had heard at the inn a few days before. It was only gossip but there's no smoke without fire.'

'What gossip?' I said uneasily.

'I don't often go into the city and very rarely into an inn, but I had made a good bargain with another fellow for some wool and we went to The Swan to seal the deal over some ale. Laut came in and drew attention to himself as always, being a little louder than he needed to be and making lewd remarks to the barmaid. I said to the man I was with that this was the man my sister was due to marry, and he earnestly entreated me to break the match if I could.'

'What reason did he give?'

'He said that Laut was keen to marry so that people would stop looking into his friendship with another man.'

'Tolmund?'

'I don't know his name. There's a tall, dark fellow that Laut hangs around with. I imagine he must be the one.'

'So your acquaintance claimed that Laut's only reason for marrying your sister was to disguise where his affections lay?'

'Yes. And that's what I told my parents when Anna had gone to bed. At first Father said it was just poisonous tittle-tattle, but Ma became upset and said that they could not let their daughter enter into a marriage with a man who led such a life. Anna would be humiliated if it became known that her husband preferred men to her. Father said so long as he needed her as cover he would be bound to treat her well, so she would be provided for, which was his aim in making the match. And, of course, Pa's word goes in any argument.'

I need hardly tell the educated reader that this allegation, if proved, was very serious indeed. A relationship between men was a capital offence in my homeland, and given that you seemed to get hanged for almost everything else in Moers I did not doubt that the same would apply there. No wonder that Laut wanted to protect himself against such a grave charge by marrying Anna Erler.

'And you believe your father could have been persuaded?' I asked.

'Not by me. But Ma might have talked Pa round. She sometimes did when she felt strongly about something. Tackling him head-on would not work, but usually she would wait until after church, then give him a good meal and let him sleep by the fire a while. When he woke up he was in a good mood and she might get her own way then.'

'Did you say that to your sister?'

'I didn't get the chance. I only saw her the next morning for a short while and my parents were nearby, so I couldn't say anything. If only she could have been patient!' He wept bitterly again.

'Has she told you she did it?'

'No. I haven't let her come near so that she could not do so. I thought if I didn't hear from her own lips what she had done I could be resolute, so I refused to have her here.'

It was very melancholy but I had no choice. I had to let the law take its course. I detested capital punishment, and the application of it to women in particular, though I confess that this is not very logical of me. Anna Erler had to hang, or burn, or whatever method was used in Moers to execute women who kill their parents. Whatever it was, I didn't want to watch it.

'You need to go home to attend to your farm,' I told him. 'I must keep your sister here. Promise me that you will not attempt to flee. You may have to repeat your evidence at the trial.'

Hubert nodded his acceptance, unable to speak due to his strong emotion.

'Your dog is at the Pittens' house,' I added.

There is a special type of providence that visits men occasionally and causes them to do something or other when they cannot describe why they have done it, but it turns out to be the right thing to do. I have heard of men who impulsively decided not to board a ship that subsequently sank, or who fail to eat poisoned food that they would normally devour greedily. In my case, something about what I had just said puzzled me, even though I was the one who had said it.

'Herr Erler, when you arrived home, where was the dog?'

'The dog? Tumbler?'

I could see by the look on his face that he had understood the importance of my question.

'He was not there. I've no idea where he was.'

It would have been just too coincidental that an elderly, lazy dog should have gone out of the house of his own volition at just the wrong time to prevent his owner being killed; and if he was not at home, the only other person he would willingly have gone with was Anna Erler. Perhaps, then, her story was true and she had been out all afternoon. Of course, she might have killed her parents, left their bodies there and then calmly walked into town, but was it likely that the dog would have left his master to go with her?

Now that I came to think of it, my neat hypothesis that Anna Erler was the killer had run up against the awkward little fact that Pitten's granddaughter said she heard two male voices and a female one.

But if not Anna Erler, then who? And how could I possibly prove it?

'I have changed my mind, Herr Erler. I must keep you here tonight for your own safety. And I must house you separately from your sister to prevent any allegation of collusion.'

Biesma and Fleckstein appeared quite bewildered by this turn of events, but loyally said nothing until we were back in my office. I explained my line of thought to them just as I have explained it to the reader.

'There is no time to lose,' I told them. 'Word will have got around that Anna Erler has been arrested. We have the element of surprise on our side, but I must think carefully how we should approach the one who holds the key to this horror. Fleckstein, kindly gather some soldiers. We need to have a conversation with someone and he may need some encouragement to speak to us.'

[No, Van der Meer, the dog did not kill his owners and then run away, and I do not believe for one moment that you ever thought he did. If you are facetiously commenting on my misreading of the evidence, I cannot complain. I had been a dolt, a sluggard, or whatever other unkind word you wish to use. But now it was clear to me.]

I sent for my cloak and laid the chain over it so that it could be seen perfectly clearly. I had no carriage but I was happy to walk. It was not far and I needed to clear my head, to which end I asked the others to stop talking to me while I thought hard. If I had not needed a German-speaker I should have left Fleckstein behind, while I had some respect for Biesma's intellect and I wanted him to hear first-hand what I heard so that I could have the benefit of his good counsel.

Together we marched down the hill to The Swan. When I say *we* marched I mean that the soldiers marched and we tried to keep up with them. When we reached the inn they opened the door and filed in, which led to a gratifying sudden silence. I suppose that half a dozen armed men would have that effect on any hostelry.

I followed them and was pleased to see that my supposition was right. In their usual corner I could see Tolmund and Laut.

'Good evening, Herr Laut,' I said, as cordially as I could. 'Would you come with us, please?'

'Where are you taking him?' asked Tolmund.

'To the castle, of course,' I replied.

'I'm coming too,' Tolmund said firmly.

'No, you're not,' I answered, equally firmly. 'Herr Laut will come alone. You can see him when we have questioned him.'

'What about?' asked Tolmund. There was a screechy quality to his voice, as of a man under strain.

'About the things we want to question him about,' I said. I was fairly exasperated by his questioning by then.

The soldiers pulled Laut to his feet. He said nothing but was clearly reluctant to come, so it was as well that I had six large men with weapons to persuade him. They frogmarched him outside.

It was at this point that the landlord felt he ought to say something, rather in the manner of the dog that barks when a feline interloper has already decided to leave the garden. 'You can't just come in here and take my customers away with no explanation!' he protested.

I was going to ignore him, but Fleckstein was not a man to back away from a challenge.

'If you seek an explanation, ask Herr Tolmund,' he said, leaving the landlord and all his customers looking accusingly at a rather deflated man shrivelling in the corner.

'I have nothing to say without a lawyer. I'm entitled to a lawyer,' Laut insisted.

'At your trial, of course. But at the moment you're only answering my questions.'

'Of what am I accused?'

'Tell me about your visit to the Erlers' house,' I said.

'What visit?'

'Your visit on the afternoon of their death.'

'Who says I visited?' His words were full of bravado but he wiped the palms of his hands on his breeches.

'Never mind who. Tell me about your visit.'

Of course, I had no proof that he had visited, but it seemed logical and a little bluff can reap great dividends sometimes.

'I went to call on Jungfrau Erler.'

'Uninvited?'

'Surely one does not need an invitation to visit one's intended?'

'She might have been alone, which would have been compromising for her.'

'Her mother was always there.'

'So her mother was there on that afternoon too?'

'Yes.'

'And what time would this be?'

'I can't say exactly. The early part of the afternoon.'

'Really?'

'I think so.'

'Did you meet anyone on the way who can confirm this?'

'No. But you must believe me.'

'So you were walking to the Erlers' farm along the road that leads out of the city at the same time as Anna Erler was walking along it towards the city and yet you did not see her, nor she you?'

Laut coloured. 'I may be wrong about the time. Maybe it was later than I thought.'

'I could tell you what time the Erlers must have been killed if that helps.'

'They were fine when I left!' he yelled. 'Completely unharmed.'

'What an odd thing to say!'

'Well, they were dead later, that's all I meant.'

'Indeed they were. They were dead when Hubert Erler returned. But if that's the case then he can't have killed them, quite apart from the fact that he had no motive.'

'He was found burying the bodies. Why would he do that if he was innocent?'

'Because he thought his sister had killed them. And she thought he had done it. That's why they have been silent for so long. But you and I know that neither of them did it, don't we?'

'You have no evidence against me.'

'On the contrary, I can describe the scene as if I had watched it. You arrived, and Herr Erler said he would no longer let you marry his daughter. He had heard things about you that had made him change his mind. Oh, at first he refused to act on them, but Frau Erler worked on him and brought him to her way of thinking. That's why you had a particular spite for her. He told you the marriage was cancelled, and then I expect you tried to argue, and he told you that he had half a mind to tell the authorities what he knew about you, and you could not let that happen. You and Tolmund would have been executed, so they had to be silenced. I don't suppose he would have said anything if you'd just accepted the marriage was off, but you didn't. You surprised him with a knife in the back, then turned on Frau Erler. And when they were dead you were in such a fever of excitement that you kept stabbing them. You were so angry at Frau Erler that you even lifted her skirts to stab her underneath. It wasn't enough that she was dead. She had to be humiliated too.'

Laut stared at each of us, his eyes wide open. 'No!' he shouted. 'No!'

'Then you tried to go ahead with the marriage, but of course Anna Erler can't marry you while she is in mourning, and with her parents exhumed she wasn't going to be out of mourning soon. So long as you remained unmarried you had no defence against Erler's charge, and you didn't know where he had heard that. If a man who was so cut off from town gossip had heard it who else could point an accusing finger at you? You needed to marry so tongues would stop wagging, but so many had turned you down. No wonder you didn't want a dowry. You would have paid to be allowed to marry Anna Erler.'

His head dropped onto his chest, his eyes fixed on the floor.

'The odd thing is that Anna Erler has not heard those accusations. Hubert only told his parents. He didn't need to turn his sister against you, because she never wanted to marry you anyway.'

'She did! She was fond of me.'

'Then why did she beg her parents to release her from any arrangement with you? Why did she tell her friends that she was unhappy about it? It seems the only person who didn't know it was you, but maybe you were wilfully blind to it because you needed that marriage so much.'

Laut tried to raise a little defiance. 'This is all the work of gossipmongers. I shall deny it all in court.'

'I'm sure you will. And I'm sure when we call Herr Tolmund forward to give his evidence on oath in front of the world he will be resolute in denying it. Or will he? He hasn't been very discreet, has he? And even if you are acquitted, do you think parents will want you teaching their children? But let's see what happens when Herr Tolmund comes to see you tomorrow, shall we? I'll question him as I have questioned you and let's see whether he is able to save your neck or decides to save his own.'

I had no idea what Tolmund would say. But I was fairly sure that a night in the cell would puncture Martin Laut's swelled-up indignation.

CHAPTER TWENTY-THREE

Morning came, and to nobody's surprise Herr Tolmund did not. Indeed, when my men called at his lodgings his room was completely empty. I have no doubt that he had been long since on the road to Duisburg and was lying very low somewhere and trying to find passage to some distant place.

Laut did not take that news well. 'Something has happened to him! He would not desert me. It's you! You have had him killed.'

'I don't have anyone killed,' I replied. 'If a court decides that someone should die, that is not my will but theirs. But it seems you are quite alone, and Tolmund does not intend to speak up for you.'

'You have prevented him. I shall say so in court.'

'Say what you will. It will not save you. And I must urge you, as you value your immortal soul, to confess what you have done. I am human and therefore may err, but one day you will stand before a greater judge, one whose verdicts are always correct and one whose mercy depends upon confession and repentance.'

It is very easy to maintain some swagger before men, but few with any wits about them can ever be indifferent to the prospect of an eternity of punishment, and I saw Laut quail at the thought.

'God is merciful but it is for Him and Him alone to determine when people like Herr and Frau Erler should die, and He will deal sharply with those who usurp His prerogative in that, don't you think? If I were so minded I could send for the executioner to put you to the instruments of torture and you would suffer a couple of hours of the worst misery you had ever experienced; and yet that will be as nothing to what awaits you from now till the end of time.'

Laut crumpled. If only my undergraduates were as responsive to my words as he was. He did not confess to me, but asked that a priest might come to him, and from that moment he made no reply to the charges but wept and sighed.

Laut came to trial the following day. Hubert and Anna Erler told their stories, and Laut made a half-hearted attempt to justify himself but it took the jury of seven men no time at all to advise me to find him guilty. I had empanelled a jury to guard against allegations that I had rigged his trial.

No sooner was their verdict delivered than Fleckstein was chirping in my ear like a canary. 'The customary sentence is death, Governor.'

Men had died as a result of my enquiries before, but I had never been the one sentencing them. I was tempted to recuse myself and let Fleckstein do it, but that would have been a dereliction of duty. Like it or not, if that is what the law says, a magistrate must follow it.

'Martin Laut, you have three days to put your soul in order, then the customary sentence will be carried out.'

I rose, they all bowed to me, then I left the room, and rushed to the privy to vomit.

It was bad enough having to sentence him. Three days later I had to watch the sentence being carried out. Laut was terrified and begged for mercy as he was bound, then led to the square where he was subjected to the taunts of the populace. Some of their comments bordered on the obscene.

I stood on the front of the scaffold and raised my hands for silence which, after a while, and after a fashion, I received. 'This man is about to pay the penalty for his crimes. Allow him some peace to prepare for the ordeal of meeting his maker.'

I did not see where the turnip came from, but the soldiers did and led a man away. I pardoned him later that afternoon.

Laut was made to climb the ladder and the rope was placed around his neck, then, about halfway through the priest's recitation of a psalm, the executioner must have pushed him off the ladder and Laut was spinning in the air. I can tell you no more. I had kept my eyes firmly fixed on the weather-cock on the building behind so as not to see what was happening.

After a few minutes Biesma turned to me to speak. 'Come, Governor, it is done. Let us go inside again.'

By that time my carriage had returned and Himst reported that Alida Krul was safely in the convent. Princess Mary wrote to tell me that her husband had been victorious without, so far as she knew, any effusion of blood, King James having fled to France and abandoned his kingdom. William had sent for her and she was to be crowned Queen, but she was determined that he should also be crowned King for, she said, it was improper for a wife to have her husband as a subject.

She had not forgotten her promise to me. I was invited to nominate someone to replace me. I was sorely tempted to give the job to Biesma because it would discomfit Fleckstein enormously, but did Biesma want it? I asked him, and he did not. Instead he sought leave to go to a monastery in Flanders, so I gave him some money for the journey and thanked him for his service, giving him a testimonial in case it was any use. Fleckstein was made sole secretary, and as for the Governorship, Mary sent a minor nobleman from our country who had studied law at Leiden, so he was obviously the best man for the job. When he arrived I enjoyed an evening with him and then departed at cock-crow the next day in case William and Mary changed their minds.

What other loose ends are there?

Pringle wrote to me to say that he was disappointed that there had been no real fighting, it having been clear to the King that people were deserting his cause in such numbers that resistance was futile. The King had escaped to France, William having carefully ensured that he could do so, since he had no wish to be forced into some parody of a trial of a King, which might only give his new subjects ideas in the future. Pringle himself had been promoted and given a command in England but was being sent to his homeland of Scotland to ensure the loyalty of the people there.

Franz Kirschbaum diligently set about writing the history of the county of Moers but inconveniently died of smallpox when he had only reached the year 950. To the best of my knowledge nobody has completed the work.

On my return to Leiden, my carriage drew up outside the Academy building on the Rapenburg and I supervised the unloading of my effects. The Rector was obliged to find me new rooms, since he had allocated mine to another man, and to my delight the new chambers were more commodious and nearer the library. While the porters installed my possessions there, I went to the refectory for some refreshment.

Mechtild looked up as I walked in and in a few seconds I was engulfed in starched apron and soft flesh as she hugged me.

'Now, sit you down there by the fire while I fetch ale and cakes, and then you must tell me all about it,' she said. Albrecht, whose arm had now healed quite well, brought me a slice of beef which was only slightly charred, and I told them all I have told you.

'And so,' I concluded, 'thus ended my one and only experience of governing a people.'

'I don't know about that,' said Albrecht. 'If the Stadhouder is to live in England with the Princess he'll need someone to run these provinces.'

I spent the rest of the night in Steen's Inn hoping William had not thought of that.

A NOTE TO THE READER

Dear Reader,

One of the most gratifying things about writing this series is that occasionally friends, especially Dutch ones, slip me snippets of information that help me to craft a story, and this book is an excellent example of that.

For the core elements of the plot I am indebted to Professor Dr Marcel Wissenburg, of Radboud University in Nijmegen, who drew my attention to William's personal ownership of Moers, and that William cunningly assembled his army at Nijmegen, which would make almost any observer believe that he had designs on Cologne and France rather than England, then moved them westward to the coast in an astonishingly quick time. Of course, what I make of these facts is entirely my own fault and Professor Wissenburg bears no responsibility for my fictional treatment of them. Equally, may I gently remind reviewers that this is not a history book and that Mercurius is allowed his own prejudices and errors.

It has often struck me as odd that in most detective stories the detective has only one case at a time. I have been as guilty of that as any, though I plead that Mercurius is an amateur. Those readers familiar with the Judge Dee books of Robert H. van Gulik will know that the Asian detective may not be so lucky. At any event, this was a chance to see how much Mercurius could handle at once, set against a rapidly shifting historical background.

I think it is important to provide interested readers with a list of some of the sources for each book. For this one, these include: Hans Goedkoop and Kees Zandvliet, *The Dutch Golden*

Age; James C. Kennedy, *A Concise History of The Netherlands*; Steve Pincus, *1688: The First Modern Revolution*; Julian Whitehead, *Espionage in the Divided Stuart Dynasty*; Michael L. Wilson, *Happy and Glorious: The Revolution of 1688* and David Womersley, *James II*.

So far as I know, this is the last time we shall meet Captain James Pringle (though I have been wrong about such predictions in the past) so it is worth recording here that he passed unscathed through the Battle of the Boyne and then returned to Scotland to marry a young lady with whom he had two sons, Alexander (1692–1740) and William (1694–1776), and lived to see them enter the army in the service of the Hanoverian kings. Indeed, William had the distinction of fighting against both the Old and the Young Pretender before writing his memoirs, which remain unpublished but which contain fascinating lists of contemporaries that he thought should have been hanged. It was while recording his strong views on the "ungrateful colonials" of America that he suffered a fatal stroke.

As for the enigmatic Tap, Mercurius was right to doubt his status as a manservant. He had, indeed, been one before becoming Pringle's valet. Pringle had trained him to become a first-class spy. He had been selected for this mission because Pringle wanted Mercurius to have a bodyguard, whether he wanted one or not. After this adventure he rejoined Pringle in Scotland and was often to be found in the inns of Edinburgh getting men drunk and encouraging them to talk too freely.

The astute reader will have noticed that with the passage of time Mercurius is becoming a little more cantankerous. I hope that despite this he will find time to dictate more adventures to Van der Meer, and that the poor scribe will continue to resist the entirely understandable temptation to throttle his master.

If you have enjoyed this novel, I'd be really grateful if you would leave a review on **Amazon** and **Goodreads**. I love to hear from readers, so please keep in touch through **Facebook, Threads** or **Twitter/X**, or leave a message on my **website**. I'd love you to subscribe to my newsletter there.

Dank je wel!

Graham Brack

SAPERE
BOOKS

Printed in Great Britain
by Amazon